While Carrie and Garvey and their families and friends are fictional, the events they lived through were real. After the flu epidemic in the winter of 1918–19, many children were left with only one parent or with no parents at all. They were taken in by other relatives, put in foster families, or adopted. Many times, brothers and sisters were separated from each other.

At the same time, the Ku Klux Klan grew throughout the country—not just in the South. In 1923–24, when this story takes place, there were ten chapters of the Klan in Minneapolis alone. The Ku Klux Klan hated African-Americans, Jews, Roman Catholics, and immigrants. They burned crosses in people's yards, vandalized their property, and in some cases beat them up or even killed them.

The Klan and people who share their views are still active. Like Carrie and Garvey, we must stand up against their evil beliefs and show God's love to everyone.

SISTERS IN TIME

Carrie's
Courage

BATTLING THE POWERS OF BIGOTRY

NORMA JEAN LUTZ

BARBOUR
PUBLISHING

Carrie's
Courage

© 2005 by Norma Jean Lutz

ISBN 1-59310-656-4

Cover design by Lookout Design Group, Inc.

Published by Barbour Publishing, Inc., P.O. Box 719, Uhrichsville, Ohio 44683
www.barbourbooks.com

Our mission is to publish and distribute inspirational products offering exceptional value and biblical encouragement to the masses.

 Member of the
Evangelical Christian
Publishers Association

Printed in the United States of America.
5 4 3 2 1

CONTENTS

CHAPTER 1

In the Attic

Caroline Ruhle pulled a small tablecloth from the old steamer trunk and shook out the wrinkles. As she did, her friend Violet sneezed three times in a row, making Carrie laugh.

"Sorry, Vi. That cloth must have been dustier than I thought," she said.

The air in the attic was heavy and still from the summer heat. The dust they were stirring up floated about their heads, going nowhere. Violet pulled a flowered handkerchief from her dress pocket and blew her nose. "I don't mind," she said. "An attic is supposed to be dusty. That's what makes it so much fun."

Carrie stood back a moment, surveying the place they'd cleared so they could play house. Pointing to a large, flat-topped trunk, she said, "Since this is the only trunk we can't open, and since it's flat, we'll use it for our table."

"Good idea," Vi agreed. "And the wooden crates can be our chairs."

While Carrie spread out the cloth, Vi dragged the boxes over to the trunk. "This high chair will be for one of the dolls," Vi said. She ran her fingers over the chipped paint of an old wooden high chair. "We'll put your doll in here. She'll be the toddler, and my doll will be the baby." Pushing her damp copper-colored curls out of her face, she glanced about the room. "There," she said, pointing to an old discarded cradle tucked up under the eaves. "We'll put my doll in the cradle."

"Bring it over," Carrie said. "Then we'll dig into the other trunks and choose our dress-up clothes."

Of all the places in the vast Victorian home that belonged to Vi's great-aunt, the girls loved the attic best of all. Although Carrie and Vi had been friends all last school year, it had only been in the last few weeks that they'd discovered the attic. And what a discovery it had been!

Up here they could play for hours, and no one bothered them. The place was full of discarded furniture, portraits, old clothes, and forgotten—but fascinating—mementos. Bare lightbulbs hung from the rafters on long cords, lights that were needed that afternoon as the skies outside darkened, promising a summer rainstorm.

Vi half dragged, half carried the wooden cradle away from the wall to their pretend tearoom. As she did, it made a terrible scraping noise. "I hope this doesn't disturb Aunt Oriel's afternoon nap," she said.

Carrie set out their doll dishes on the cloth-covered trunk. "Vi, don't you think it's strange that this is the only trunk in the whole attic that's locked?" she wondered aloud.

Vi sat down on a crate, breathing heavily from exertion. "I never really thought about it. I'm just glad all the others are open."

Fiddling with the rusty clasp, Carrie tried it one more time to see if it would open—as if she hadn't already attempted to do so a hundred times. Just as before, it wouldn't budge. "Perhaps it's full of old diaries and journals," she said dreamily. "What fun it would be to read an old diary."

"Money would be better. Lots of money." Vi rose from her

resting spot and moved the cradle close by the trunk and put the doll in it.

"Money's not very sentimental."

"No," Vi said, "but it could buy some nice school clothes. And speaking of clothes. . ." She opened one of the big trunks and started pulling out fancy dresses and hats and shoes. "Let's choose which we'll wear today."

Carrie joined her friend in selecting the most beautiful gowns, but she was still thinking about what Vi had said about money. Money was never talked about at the Ruhle household. Her father, Glendon Ruhle, had a great job with the *Minneapolis Tribune*, and there was always more than enough money. But for Vi and her brother, Nathaniel, orphans living with an aged aunt who was practically a recluse, perhaps money *was* a problem. She felt sorry that she'd not thought of it before.

"Pin me here," Vi said. She turned about in a long, rust-colored dress and handed Carrie a safety pin. Carrie pinned it at the waist, making the gown fit better.

"I'm so glad your aunt Oriel doesn't mind our playing with her old things." On her head, Carrie set a plum-colored, wide-brimmed hat that was adorned with three large ostrich plumes. The plumes were dyed to match the hat perfectly. Looking in the dingy mirror of an old bureau, she tucked her dark pigtails up under the hat.

"Actually, we don't really know if she approves or not," Vi said. "We haven't seen her for weeks."

"Weeks?"

"Weeks. She just shuts herself up in the east wing of the house where her bedroom, library, and drawing room all adjoin. You'd think if she really wanted Nate and me to live here, she'd come out once in a while."

"Don't forget," Carrie reminded her, "she is awfully old. Old people act strangely sometimes." Turning from the mirror, she asked, "Doesn't she ever talk to anyone? How lonely that must be."

"I suppose she talks to Opal when she takes Aunt Oriel's meals in and out."

"What would your aunt do without Opal?" Carrie asked.

"What would *we* do without Opal?" Vi said as she wrapped a long pink feather boa around her neck, giving it a little extra fling for emphasis. "Opal's the one who said we could play up here."

Opal Howerton had been in the employ of the Simmonses' household for decades—ever since the days when there was a full staff. Now filling the roles of cook, housekeeper, and nanny, Opal was as warm and caring to the Bickerson children as Mrs. Simmons was distant and aloof.

Vi leaned into an open trunk and pulled out a pair of dainty dancing slippers. Slipping her feet into them, she said, "Carrie, if I tell you something, promise you won't tell anyone."

"You know I'd never tell, Vi."

She came closer and lowered her voice, even though there wasn't another soul within hearing distance. "Sometimes I think that after Mother and Father died of the influenza, Aunt Oriel never really wanted us to come and live with her."

"Oh, Vi. That couldn't be true. You and Nate are no trouble—"

"We're not really related to her, you know." Vi lifted the skirts of her dress and stepped over to their pretend table. Sitting on a crate, she acted as though she were pouring tea from the teapot of their toy china tea set.

"But you call her *aunt*."

"She's only our aunt by marriage. She was married to my grandfather's brother, James Simmons."

Carrie picked up her doll from the high chair, sat opposite Vi, and pretended to feed the baby. "Marriage or no, she's still your aunt."

Vi sighed. "I suppose. But I can't help but wonder. . . ."

Carrie had never heard Vi talk like this before. Her heart ached for her friend. She'd always known it must be dreadful to have both parents die. But to think her aunt didn't want her must be almost more than a person could bear.

A tapping on the second-floor door at the foot of the stairs interrupted her thoughts. "Girls," came Opal's voice. "Come open the door. I have a tray."

Vi's eyes lit up. "Ooo–eee. She's brought us a snack." Vi jumped up so fast that she nearly stumbled over her long skirts.

Carrie giggled. "Careful on the stairs," she warned.

In a matter of minutes, a winded Opal was setting the tray on the trunk. There were cookies and little cakes, along with a pitcher of juice and two tumblers.

"Looks as though you girls are having tons of fun," the hefty lady quipped, giving her broad smile that made dimples appear in her round face.

"We are, Opal," Vi assured her. "But we'll have even more fun now with all this food."

Opal nodded, wiping sweaty hands on her soiled apron. "I thought you might." Taking the corner of her apron, she touched it to her forehead and reddened cheeks.

"Opal," Carrie said, "is there a key to this trunk?" She patted the giant trunk that served as their makeshift table.

Opal shook her head. "Don't think so. I've been around here almost thirty years, and there's never been a key that I remember."

"What do you suppose is in it?" Carrie asked.

"More stuff," she said with a chuckle, waving her hand at the expanse of the attic. "Just like all this here stuff!" The housekeeper reached out and gave Violet a loving pat and then turned to go. "Now you girls have a nice time playing. I'm getting me down out of this stifling oven."

"Thanks for the snack, Opal," Vi said.

"Yes. Thanks so much," Carrie echoed.

Opal stopped at the head of the attic stairway, fanning her face with the tail of her apron. "Think nothing of it. My pleasure. Be sure you girls put everything back in its proper place when you're finished."

"We will," Vi promised.

When Opal was partway down the stairs, she hollered back up, "If the boys come back, just send them to the kitchen for their snack." She was talking about Vi's brother, Nathaniel, and Carrie's cousin, Garvey Constable—an ornery pair if there ever was one. Garvey was ten, the same age as Vi and Carrie. Nate was a year older.

"We'll tell them," Vi answered, then turned to Carrie and said with a grin, "If they don't have sense enough to go to the kitchen for themselves, should I have to tell them?"

Carrie laughed.

After several cookies had been devoured, Carrie said, "Now, let's take the babies and go up to the turret." The turret was the highest part of the big old house, and Carrie loved the small cozy room that looked out over the neighborhood in all directions.

Vi didn't feel the same about the turret. "It'll be hotter up there than down here," she said. "And going up those narrow stairs in our dresses and shoes will be a real chore." Vi paused. "Tell you what. You take your baby and go to the turret if you want. We'll pretend you're traveling to a far country."

Carrie smiled. "I'll get the baby ready right away," she said and headed toward the stairs. It *was* difficult to maneuver the stairs in her long dress. And it was hot, just as Vi said, but Carrie loved the octagonal room.

From its vantage point, she could see past the row of stately homes on the block clear to the sandlot on Franklin Avenue where the neighborhood boys had a rousing baseball game going. If she squinted, she could make out which one was Garvey and which was Nate.

Summer flowers were in full bloom, and the formal gardens located in back of the Carrutherses' house next door were a picture of orderly beauty. Jonathan Carruthers, a banker, was the wealthiest man in the neighborhood.

Oriel Simmons's back lot was a different story. While it was kept mowed, that was about the extent of the upkeep. There were no flowers and probably had been none for several years.

Carrie leaned against one of the windows and watched the thickening storm clouds slowly move over the city. If she lived in this house, she'd spend all her waking hours in this special room, writing her poems. That wasn't to say that she couldn't write poetry in her own room at home. After all, she had no brothers or sisters to bother her. But the turret. . . The turret, perched high atop the Simmonses' house was special somehow—so secluded, so old-fashioned, and so loaded with character. She whispered softly to herself:

> *Rain, rain, rain, rain,*
>   *Splashing down my windowpane.*

Just then, Vi called up the stairs, "Isn't your trip about over? It's getting lonely down here."

"Coming," Carrie answered. As she turned to go, the patter of rain sounded against the windows. She'd have to finish her rain poem later.

"Listen to that, Vi," she said as she descended back into the attic. "Doesn't the rain sound lovely? Rain makes the attic seem even more cozy."

"Cozy, yes," Vi agreed. "But it also means the boys' ball game will be rained out."

Carrie wrinkled her nose. "You're right. I hadn't thought of that."

"If they come up here, they have to play what we're playing. No changing. Agreed?"

"Agreed," Carrie said with as much firmness in her voice as she could muster. Actually, it was difficult to be firm at all with Garvey. Her cousin was forever cutting up and acting silly.

The rain grew from fat drops to a steady drumming on the roof, making little rivulets on the windows.

"Let's both be rich ladies," Vi suggested, changing the subject.

"Oh, let's," Carrie agreed. "The governess will come and care for the children, and we'll go to the opera. A special car will come with a chauffeur to take us."

Vi giggled. "Like Mr. Carruthers next door?"

Carrie waved her hand. "Oh, pooh. His old car is nothing to the one that will come to fetch us."

Vi laughed even more. "Ours will be like the Pierce Arrow that Greta Garbo drives."

Violet loved to read movie magazines, and that's where she had seen a photo of Greta Garbo in her custom-designed Pierce Arrow.

"Yes! That's it," Carrie agreed. "Like Greta's car."

A slam of a door and heavy footsteps on the attic stairs interrupted their game. Vi rolled her eyes. "Guess who?" she said.

"Here we are," came Garvey's voice before his head appeared at the stairwell. "Now the fun can begin."

CHAPTER 2

Sonny's Radio

Like two frisky colts with an overabundance of energy, Garvey and Nate barreled into the attic room, rain-soaked and mud-splattered. Nate yanked off his ball cap, underneath which his thatch of sandy hair was matted from the rain. "Glad to see us?" he said, grinning.

"How did you get by Opal looking like that?" Vi demanded. "You could have at least changed into something clean and dry."

"Opal's busy in the kitchen. We came up the front stairs," Nate said.

"And what's wrong with the way we look?" Garvey demanded. "We'll dry off."

Vi leaned over to Carrie. "At least they left their bat and ball and mitts downstairs."

Carrie snickered. "Wonder of wonders," she remarked.

Nate sat down on the wooden floor to tie a long, trailing shoe-string. "If it'd been up to us, we'd have kept right on playing, rain or no. Right, Garvey?"

"Right as rain!" he quipped, then laughed at his own bad joke, making the girls groan. "We were whipping them something awful. I smacked a homer that would have made Babe Ruth smile."

"Garvey," Carrie said, "it's not polite to brag on yourself."

"But he did," Nate insisted. "He slammed a good one and sent three runners in. Me included."

"Well, we're not interested in baseball," Vi announced. "If you're staying up here, you have to be the husbands."

Now it was the boys' turn to groan.

"We're rich ladies," Carrie explained. "And these," she added, pointing to the dolls, "are our children."

"No need to pretend there," Nate said to Carrie. "You already *are* rich." He was still sitting on the floor, his wet hair all askew and his arms clasped around his knees.

"Why, Nathaniel Bickerson," Vi chided her brother, "that wasn't a very nice tone of voice."

Garvey was digging through one of the trunks. He stopped and turned to Nate. "Hey, Nate, she's my cousin, and I can tell you she's not rich. It's just that they don't have as many mouths to feed as we do at our house."

Nate shrugged. "You both have a bunch more than we'll ever have."

Garvey threw a suit coat and an old silk-lined fedora at him. "Good grief, Nate. Stop whining. Look at all this great stuff you have to play with. We don't have anything like this at our house."

Nate caught the hat in midair. The jacket landed beside him. "But none of it's mine. It all belongs to Aunt Oriel. And Sonny, of course," he added. When he mentioned Sonny, his green eyes took on a stormy look that Carrie had seen there much too often in recent days.

Carrie knew Nate didn't care much for his aunt's seventeen-year-old grandson. But she'd never really heard such bitterness in Nate's voice before when he talked about Sonny. Sonny was an orphan, just as Nate and Violet were. Carrie had no idea how long Sonny had lived with his grandmother.

"If you're going to play," Vi said, ignoring her brother's remarks, "you have to get dressed up. The chauffeur is arriving soon, and we're all going to the opera."

"The opera? Oh, brother!" Garvey slapped his forehead. "I have a better idea than that. You three pretend you're going to a vaudeville show, and I'll be the song-and-dance man." With that, he mashed a hat on his head and twirled a pearl-headed cane in his hand.

Nate jumped up. "Great idea, Garvey. Let's string up twine from that nail by the window to that hall tree over there. We'll hang a sheet over it and make a stage."

Carrie glanced at Vi. "They're doing it again," she said. It seemed like the boys were always ruining their games.

"Garvey, look." Nate was pointing to the girls' empty food tray. "They had a snack, and we missed out."

"There's more where that came from," Vi told him. "Opal said for you to come down to the kitchen anytime."

"I'll go down," Garvey said to Nate. "You fix our stage curtain, and I'll be back in a minute. With food, of course!" Down the stairs he went—just as noisily as he'd come up.

Nate found a coil of twine used to tie up old boxes. "Garvey truly did hit a great homer," he said as he stood on a crate and tied one end of the twine to the nail. "He's a doggone good player."

Carrie looked over at Vi, and Vi rolled her eyes. All the two boys ever thought about or talked about was baseball. Carrie knew perfectly well that Nate was every bit as good as Garvey. Even better. But they bragged on each other constantly.

"Are we ready to go to the show?" Vi asked, ignoring Nate's baseball comment altogether. "Or shall we change our frocks?"

"By all means, let's change," Carrie said, waving a long silk glove in the air.

After a few moments, they had the first dresses off and new ones pulled on and were pinning one another. Suddenly a horrendous noise sounded from behind them, like a loud slam and then a guttural growl. Vi jumped and gasped. Carrie screamed and whirled around, her heart pounding in her throat.

There stood Garvey with an old sheet draped over his head. He'd snuck up the back way. Now the two boys were laughing hysterically. "Did you see them jump?" Garvey said, pulling the sheet off.

"Both of them," Nate gasped as he held his sides. He had to get down off the crate because he was laughing so hard. "Jumped about a mile in the air."

Now Vi was laughing, too. "Garvey, you crazy guy. You scared me all right. You're always up to some kind of mischief."

Carrie didn't think it was so funny. Her heart was still pounding like a trip-hammer. She didn't always care for Garvey's antics, but what could she say? Nate and Vi never seemed to mind. In fact, no matter how corny Garvey acted, they always laughed.

"How'd you know, Nate?" Vi wanted to know. "Why didn't he scare you?"

"He signaled to me on his way out. Pretty funny, huh?"

"Those back stairs are a clever setup," Garvey said. "I love this swell old house."

"Hey," Nate said, "what about our food?"

"Oh yeah," Garvey said, grinning. "I left it on the landing."

In no time, the boys wolfed down their cookies and juice and turned their attention back to the makeshift curtain.

Garvey helped as they strung the twine from the nail over to the hooks of a discarded hall tree. They used the sheet Garvey had worn for his awful joke, spreading it over the twine for a curtain.

As they did, Nate happened to look out the window.

"Well, would you look over there," he said, his hands on his hips. "There's Mr. Carruthers's new chauffeur! Sonny says he's a Russian Jew. A poor immigrant Jew."

Garvey dropped the twine and craned over to peer down at the neighbor's house.

Vi was putting on yet another elegant hat. After adjusting it, she said, "I want to see." Lifting her long skirts, she scurried over to where the boys were gawking.

Carrie wondered what all the fuss was about. It wasn't as if they'd never seen Mr. Carruthers's chauffeurs before. He'd been through several in the past couple years.

"Come look, Carrie," Vi said, motioning.

Carrie sighed. She lifted her long skirt and traipsed to the window as she'd been asked. Looking through the window, which was rain-streaked on the outside and dusty on the inside, she saw the Carrutherses' elegant Packard car. Slowly, the car moved from the large three-car garage around to the portico. The front of the car was open, the back enclosed, leaving the uniformed driver in the rain—which had slacked off to barely a sprinkle. Carrie leaned closer to look down, but the driver, dressed in a trim uniform complete with visored cap and jodhpurs, didn't look so different. Nothing special set him apart.

The car stopped beneath the open portico. The driver stepped out and, standing straight and tall, opened the car door for Mr. Carruthers to enter. As usual, Mr. Carruthers was dressed to the teeth in his tailored three-piece suit. The chauffeur then got back in the front seat, and they drove away.

"Jewish," Nate said with a sneer. "He probably wears one of those little beanie things on his head under that chauffeur's cap."

"It's called a *yarmulke*," Garvey said.

"Yeah," Nate agreed. "One of those."

"So what if he does?" Carrie commented. She didn't particularly like the way Nate was talking about this poor man. "Mr. Carruthers doesn't seem to care if he's Jewish or not."

"Sonny says the Jews should stay in their part of town," Nate said.

"But that's his home," Carrie countered, pointing to the Carrutherses' place. "Mr. Carruthers's chauffeurs always live above the garage. Besides, what does Sonny Simmons know anyway?"

Sometimes Nate seemed not to care a thing about what Sonny said or did. Other times, he acted as though what Sonny said was law. How confusing.

"Are we going to finish our game?" Vi asked, moving back to their tea table, "or are we going to stare out an old window all day?"

"Yes," Carrie agreed. "If you're going to make a stage, then make a stage. We're ready to go to the show."

She figured playing vaudeville would be better than staring at the neighbors.

Garvey tossed Nate the fedora, and Nate caught it and put it on at a rakish angle.

Just then, from outside came a familiar chugging and popping noise. There was no mistaking the sound of Sonny's old jalopy that he'd souped up. The old car was the noisiest one in the entire neighborhood. Which seemed to suit Sonny just fine.

"Oh my!" Nate exclaimed, still gaping out the window. "Looky there. Sonny's gone and got himself a radio set!" He pulled off the hat and gave it a spin, making it sail toward an open trunk. It landed perfectly inside. "A real honest-to-goodness radio set!"

He grabbed Garvey's arm. "Come on, Garvey. We gotta see

this. Maybe he'll let us have a look."

"Or a listen," Garvey added, dropping the twine and tripping right on Nate's heels.

Down the stairs they went, sounding like a herd of elephants.

CHAPTER 3

Tennis Lessons

Carrie shook her head as the attic was suddenly quiet again. "Boys," she said with a sigh.

"Carrie?" Vi stood in the middle of the room, looking somewhat distracted.

"Yes?"

"I'd like to see the radio set. I've never seen one before."

"What do you mean? You've seen our radio."

Vi was pulling off her dress-up dress and putting it back into the trunk. "Your family radio is different. Sonny probably put this one together wire by wire and tube by tube."

Carrie could see it was useless to argue with her friend. Their game was over for this day. She, too, pulled off her long dress, her hat, and her shoes and put them back into the trunk.

"Hurry," Vi said. "We'll pick up the rest of the things later."

The attic stairs opened into a hallway on the second floor, where Nate and Vi's bedrooms were located. From there, they went down the back stairs, which led to the kitchen and the stairs that led to the basement. By the time they got down there, Sonny had situated the radio receiver set on a broad worktable and was fiddling with the glass tubes and hooking up wires here and there. Garvey and Nate were standing at a respectful distance, quietly watching Sonny's every move.

Sonny looked over at the girls as they entered and rolled his dark eyes. "That's all I need," he spouted. "Two more pests."

Carrie had never known Sonny to be very friendly, and today was no different. The tall, lanky boy had the disposition of a porcupine, keeping most everyone at a distance. His thick dark hair was cut high over his ears but long on top and kept falling across his forehead as he worked.

For reasons known only to Sonny, he preferred to live in the basement. Not that it was a bad place. It was fixed up as nice as any other part of the house, with paneled walls and ample lighting. It just seemed odd to Carrie that Sonny kept himself isolated in much the same way that his grandmother did. Which didn't make living here any easier for Vi and Nate.

Vi was right about the radio. It looked nothing like the mahogany console sitting in the Ruhles' living room. Sonny's radio was definitely a do-it-yourself contraption of which he was obviously very proud. On the one hand, he talked as though he wanted them to leave, but on the other, he kept fussing over the set as though he wanted them to watch.

He leaned close to the set, a weak smile playing on his usually scowling face, his dark, deep-set eyes focused in concentration.

Presently, there were scratchy sounds coming over the airwaves. After a little dial twisting, Sonny was able to bring in—through spurts of heavy static—sounds of a jazz band playing. As soon as he did, he picked up a set of headphones and put them on his ears, wiring them to the set. The music was silenced; only he could hear.

"Can we try the headphones, Sonny?" Nate asked. "Please?"

"Not on your life," Sonny answered. "You think I'd trust this delicate equipment to a bunch of little kids?" He lifted up one earphone and looked at the four of them. "You twerps are bothering me. Now scram! All of you!"

Carrie turned to go up the stairs. She wasn't used to being talked to in such a rude manner. She was the first up the steps, followed by the other three. When they were all standing in the middle of the big kitchen, she asked, "Why does he have to be so snippy?"

"He's just that way," Nate replied, pulling his ball cap on over his still-mussed-up hair. "Come on, Garvey. The sun's back out. Maybe the fellows are ready to start the game again."

"Yeah. Let's go."

"Wait just a minute." Opal stood in the kitchen doorway with her hands on her ample hips. "Did everything get picked up and put away in the attic? I seem to be missing two trays, complete with tumblers and pitchers."

Garvey groaned.

"Come on," Vi said. "Let's all pitch in." Looking over at Carrie, she said, "After we finish picking up, let's go play at the park."

Quickly the foursome ran back up to the attic, and in a matter of minutes, they'd put everything back in its rightful place. As they came back into the kitchen to put the trays in the sink, the telephone rang.

Vi ran to the wall phone in the kitchen to grab it before Opal could answer one of the extensions. Carrie wasn't sure how many telephones were in the Simmonses' house, but there were several.

"Here, Carrie," Vi said, handing the receiver off to Carrie. "It's for you."

"Me?"

"Your mother."

"Wonder what she wants?" Carrie took the phone. "Hello, Mother."

"Carrie, why aren't you here? You should be changing into your tennis togs by now. It's almost time for your lesson."

"Oh my. I completely forgot."

"Well, get home as quickly as you can. Perhaps we can still make it on time."

Carrie placed the receiver on the hook of the wall phone. Wrinkling her nose, she said, "I have to go. It's time for my tennis lesson."

"Oh yeah," Garvey said, "your tennis lesson. I was supposed to help you remember. We neither one did a very good job, did we?"

Carrie shook her head. She hated going to tennis lessons at the country club each week. It was something Mother thought would help make her a more well-rounded person. That and the elocution sessions, piano lessons, and two workshops of art appreciation. It was as though her mother was attempting to schedule Carrie's entire summer.

"I sure wish you didn't have to leave," Vi said. "Guess I'll have to go play by myself for a while."

"Sorry," Carrie said, heading out the back door. "I'd better hurry, or Mother will be upset." She waved to Vi as her friend stood on the back porch with a forlorn expression on her face.

Carrie knew Violet was often lonely, so she spent as much time with her friend as possible. And besides that, the two of them had great fun together.

As Carrie walked past the Carrutherses' place, the fancy Packard was pulling into the driveway. The new chauffeur looked over at Carrie and smiled. It was a very nice smile. It made her think of the poem in her reading book that went:

The thing that goes the farthest
Toward making life worthwhile,

That costs the least and does the most,
Is just a pleasant smile.

Carrie's house was only four blocks from the Simmonses' place, and she was home in a matter of minutes. Their Chandler Six was sitting in the driveway when Carrie arrived. Mother, dressed and ready, was pacing in the front room.

"Caroline," she said when Carrie entered. "How inconsiderate of you. Mr. Clausen will be fuming if we're late."

"Sorry, Mother. Truly I am. Sonny came in with a radio set, and we all went to look."

"Sonny Simmons?" Mother shook her head. "I don't mind you playing with the Bickerson children, but I wish you wouldn't keep company with Sonny. He's a ne'er-do-well if I ever saw one."

"Don't worry. He calls us *little kids* and chases us out."

"Good enough." Pulling on her gloves, Carrie's mother waved her toward the stairs. "Your togs are laid out on your bed. Hurry and change."

The air was muggy after the rain, and Carrie didn't feel like hurrying at all. She certainly didn't feel like playing tennis. She changed into the pleated white skirt and middy top with the navy sailor ties that hung down the front. Kicking off her play shoes, she pulled on the long cotton stockings and white canvas tennis shoes. Strands of her dark hair were falling out of her braids, but there was no time to redo them. She was out in the upstairs hall when she stopped, ran back into her room, grabbed the racquet in the corner, and ran back out again.

Mother was in the car with the motor running. Carrie jumped in, propping the racquet beside her. As they drove out toward the country club, Mother talked about the work she'd done that morning with the League of Women Voters. Carrie's mother was always off and doing with some group or other. Sometimes it was with civic groups, sometimes with the church. "We must give back to society," she'd say. "None of us can be takers only."

The country club was a long, low building made of rough native stone and surrounded by manicured golf courses. Mother pulled the Chandler Six up under a shade tree to keep it cool while they were inside. Carrie hopped out and hurried to keep in step with her mother as they went up the winding walk.

"We'll go around this way," Mother said, pointing to the side of the building. "It'll be faster."

Mr. Clausen, looking cool in his white slacks and knit shirt, was sitting at one of the little tables on the patio shaded by a yellow-and-white striped umbrella. His hair was slicked back, movie-star style, and he was sipping an iced drink. He was young and terribly good-looking. He looked nothing like the pastor he was studying to become. The part-time job at the country club was helping to put him through divinity school.

He looked up at them and smiled as they approached. He insisted he'd been waiting only a few moments and didn't seem nearly as upset as Mother had indicated he might be. To Carrie, it appeared as though he had nothing else to do.

Mother chose to wait inside out of the hot sun. "I need to make a few telephone calls," she said, giving Carrie a little wave.

This was Carrie's fourth lesson, and each time she seemed to do worse instead of better. "Today we're working on the backhand," Mr. Clausen instructed after the warm-up exercises were completed.

Carrie wondered how she could have progressed to a backhand when her serve was still quite terrible. Repeatedly, Mr. Clausen had demonstrated how to throw the tennis ball up and then swing at the ball as it came down. He made it look so easy. But she missed it more times than she hit it.

Now she listened and held the racquet just as he instructed. "The backhand, just like the forehand, begins low and ends high," Mr. Clausen told her. "Reach across like so." Standing beside her, he demonstrated the proper technique for a backhand. She wasn't sure that she would ever catch on.

After several practice swings, he moved to the other side of the net to hit a few balls. As Carrie fumbled about the court, in her mind ran the first two lines of a new poem:

Anyone for tennis?
  To me, it's just a menace!

Mr. Clausen was kind, and he seemed to sense her heart wasn't in the sport of tennis. "Think of it this way," he told her as they took a short break. "You may never play at Wimbledon, but if in a few years some handsome young fellow asks you on a tennis date, you'll at least know which end of the racquet to hold."

Carrie smiled. "Thank you, Mr. Clausen. That gives me a glimmer of hope." He handed her a towel, and she mopped at the perspiration on her forehead.

It had only been during this, her tenth summer, that Mother had begun this "well-rounded" thing for Carrie. "It's not enough to just float through life," she said. "It's important to learn a little bit about many things in order to have a well-rounded education and personality."

And before Carrie could enjoy barely a month of summer freedom, she found her free time was entangled with workshops and lessons all week long, every week. She could hardly keep the times straight. Garvey said it must be like living in a straitjacket. While his description made her smile, it was true. The endless lessons almost took all the fun out of summer.

Before practice was completed, Carrie finally executed a couple very nice serves. "Ah, good," Mr. Clausen said. "Now I'll be able to tell your mother you're coming along famously."

Carrie laughed. "Don't go overboard. No sense making her expect something that isn't there."

"You have a point," he replied.

Mother was standing out on the patio in the shade of the yellow awning as they approached. Mr. Clausen reported on Carrie's good lesson, then said, "Let me treat you and Caroline to an ice cream soda."

"Thank you, Mr. Clausen, but we've no time for sodas today. Too many things to do."

"It'd only take a few minutes," he protested. "I have a feeling Carrie would finish hers off rather quickly."

Mother put her hand on Carrie's shoulder, leading her away. "Next time, perhaps."

Carrie felt cranky and out of sorts as she climbed back into the car, which had heated up to oven temperature. How could a person have time to drive clear across town for a tennis lesson but have no time to enjoy an ice cream soda?

That made no sense to Carrie. No sense at all.

CHAPTER 4

Family Gathering

The Constable house was full to overflowing as it usually was on Sunday afternoons. This was Carrie's favorite time of the week, when she could be with all her cousins and aunts and uncles.

Garvey's family and Carrie's family attended the same church, and Garvey was even in Carrie's Sunday school class. The Maurers—Aunt Elena, Uncle Hans, and Cousin Edith—attended a different church in another part of town, but they usually came to the Constables' for dinner as well.

The Maurers' oldest daughter, Liese, sometimes came with her husband, Donald, and their two little ones. Carrie loved being around the babies. She liked to pretend they were her little brother and sister. Sometimes it got a little lonely being an only child.

Garvey always told her she should be thankful to be the only one. "Larry teases me," he'd say, "Gloria bosses me, and little Felix gets into my stuff. It's no fun at all." But in spite of what he said, Carrie knew they had good times together.

Carrie was sitting on the floor in the front room. "See if he'll come to me," she said to Liese. Tall, slender Liese was sitting in the rocking chair with baby Joseph in her lap. At almost a year old, Joseph was learning to take his first baby steps. Liese set him down, and Carrie held out her hands. Joseph cooed and smiled, then took a couple unsteady steps before practically falling into her lap. Carrie held him close, cuddling him and inhaling the sweet baby smell.

"Oh, I love you, little Joey," she said as she rocked him.

"I think his first words are going to be *Cousin Carrie*," Liese joked.

"I'd like that," Carrie answered. "I'd like that a lot."

"You'd like what?" Garvey's thirteen-year-old sister, Gloria, had just come out of the kitchen where the women were still cleaning up the dinner dishes.

"I'd like for Joey's first words to be *Cousin Carrie*."

Gloria smiled as she sat down on the floor next to Carrie. "He's growing so fast," she said, giving Joseph an affectionate pat on his thick diapers. "I can hardly believe he's walking already."

"Watch him," Carrie said, setting Joseph back up on his feet.

As Gloria held out her arms, he toddled to her, laughing and cooing as he went.

Behind them, the men were talking in earnest about radios. Fifteen-year-old Larry was sitting with them, intent on being included in the adult conversation.

Carrie had never known it to fail. Whenever the family gathered, the men were always debating about some issue or another. Uncle Kenneth, a physician, and Carrie's father, a newspaper reporter, seldom agreed on anything. Uncle Hans, a foreman in the flour mill, was the quieter one. While Uncle Hans had definite opinions, he was never quite as vocal as the other two. Liese's husband, Donald Albright, joined in, as well.

Garvey came in the room just then, all hot and sweaty from playing in the yard. Four-year-old Felix was right on his heels. Felix was Garvey's little shadow, following him wherever he went.

Uncle Kenneth looked up from fiddling with dials on his console radio. "Garvey," he said, "you're getting grass all over the floor. If you don't want your mother to throttle you, I suggest you go to the porch and brush it off."

"Yes, sir," Garvey answered.

"Yes, sir," Felix echoed. The two went back outside again.

"As I was saying," Uncle Ken said to his brothers-in-law, "there should be absolutely no commercialism on the radio."

Sizzly static sounded through the speakers until he got the radio tuned in. A voice came on announcing an orchestral number.

"I don't agree," Father countered. "It's already been proven that when a product is mentioned on the air, sales immediately shoot up. The potential to sell products on the airwaves is too great to discount."

Uncle Ken shook his head in his solemn way. "Why, Glendon, the airwaves belong to everyone. It's like a public trust." Static sizzled once more, and Uncle Ken worked the dials again until the noise cleared. "If we let money-hungry corporations put their commercials on the air, radio will become distasteful to everyone."

"Nonsense," Father retorted. "What better way for listeners to learn about new products?"

Uncle Hans held Liese's three-year-old daughter, Patricia, in his lap. The little girl was nearly asleep. Carrie could tell her uncle was thinking, but he kept his comments to himself.

"The radio weather reports are a great help to the pilots out at the airport," Larry put in. Larry worked at the Twin Cities Flying Field and loved everything about airplanes and flying. "But," he continued, "I don't see how announcers and radio personalities can be paid if commercials aren't allowed. Where will the money come from?"

"See there, Kenneth?" Father quipped. "Your son understands the concept clearly enough."

Joseph toddled back to Carrie, and she placed him on his back on the floor, tickling his tummy and making him gurgle. As she did, she made up a little ditty:

Hie–di–ho and away we go,
Listening to our radio.
Commercials yes, commercials no
Pay big bucks, we'll air your show.

Now it was Uncle Ken's turn to laugh. To Father, he said, "Excuse me, Glendon, but it sounds like your daughter understands the concept. It's all about big bucks."

Now everyone was laughing, even Father. Carrie was blushing. She hadn't meant to make a point. She just liked the rhythm of the words.

"Back to what I was saying," Father continued. "The *Detroit News* has set up a radio station right in their newspaper office. Obviously, they see radio as the perfect news medium—an extension of the newspaper, if you will."

"That makes sense," Donald Albright put in. "Listeners can get bits of headlines on the radio and then get the details from the newspaper."

"Exactly," Father agreed. "I'm trying to talk my boss into sending me to Detroit to see how their system is set up."

"Why don't you just fly to Detroit?" Larry asked. He always thought of travel in terms of flying. "I could help you hire a plane and a pilot."

Carrie looked over at her father to see his reaction. Glendon

Ruhle loved new adventures, which is why he was such a keen newshound. She saw his eyes light up at the prospect of taking an airplane trip.

"I hadn't thought of that, Larry. Flying to Detroit would certainly be the quickest way. How much would it cost?"

"Probably just the price of fuel," Larry told him. "Most of the pilots out at the field jump at a chance to fly—anywhere, anytime."

Father nodded. "You find out, and let me know."

Just then the women came in from the kitchen, and all talk of airplanes and radios stopped. Mother sat down near Father and Uncle Kenneth. To her older brother, she said, "Frances just told me that Jonathan Carruthers has hired a Jewish immigrant as his new chauffeur. A single man with no family."

Uncle Ken nodded. "I heard."

"Good for him," Uncle Hans spoke up. Uncle Hans, who'd known much persecution both as a labor union man and as a German during the war, was always in favor of the underdog, the down-and-outer.

"I hope he knows what he's doing," Father said. "The Klan activities in the city have increased in the past few months. They don't much like the Jews—or the people who have anything to do with Jews."

Seventeen-year-old Edie, the youngest Maurer daughter, entered the room just in time to hear that last remark. She seated herself on the floor with Gloria and Carrie. "Klan members don't seem to like anyone different than they are," she stated flatly.

"I saw him," Carrie said.

"Saw whom?" Aunt Frances asked.

"The chauffeur."

"You saw Yerik Levinsky?" she asked.

Carrie nodded. "If that's the name of the chauffeur. I was playing with Violet Bickerson next door. I saw him bringing the Packard home after taking Mr. Carruthers somewhere."

"Well, tell us," Edie said, leaning forward. "What did he look like?"

Carrie thought a minute. "He has a nice smile."

"Well, there you have it," Uncle Kenneth said. "Could we be suspicious of someone who has a nice smile?"

Uncle Hans shook his head. "People who live with suspicion don't look at smiles—or any other virtue for that matter."

"Papa's right," Edie agreed. "The Klan just took up where the hate from the war left off."

Carrie had heard a few things about the Ku Klux Klan. None of it was good. She knew there were groups of them all around the country and that the members wore white robes with big pointed hoods. Father had said they hid because they were ashamed of their acts.

There were reports that Klan members were against people of other faiths, such as the Jews and the Catholics, and people of other races, such as those with black skin. That sure seemed like a lot of people to hate. How could they keep it all straight? Mostly, Carrie couldn't figure out how a Jewish immigrant could be a threat to someone like the Ku Klux Klan.

"Jews have often been discriminated against," Uncle Ken stated, "but we mustn't forget that they are our heritage. They are God's Chosen, the Bible says. We, on the other hand, are merely grafted in."

The announcer on the radio advertised an upcoming jazz band. Uncle Ken reached over and turned it off. He didn't much care for jazz music.

After everyone's dinner had settled, they went outside for a game of croquet. Carrie gladly took care of Joseph while Liese joined in the action.

"Since Carl and Oscar aren't here," Liese said, referring to her two brothers, "I have to defend the family name!"

Carrie sat on the grass for a while, watching the game. When the baby got fussy, she went inside to the kitchen, where Aunt Frances was getting the custard ready to make homemade ice cream.

"Carrie," said her aunt, "I'm going to keep Patty and Joey for Liese one day next week. Why don't you ask your mother if you can come over and help me?" Aunt Frances knew quite well how much Carrie loved being around the babies. Liese's mother, Aunt Elena, worked as a typist in a freight office, so she wasn't available to keep the babies during the day like Aunt Frances was.

Carrie sat down in one of the kitchen chairs and gave Joseph his bottle, rocking him as he fed. "I have something scheduled most every day of the week," she said with a sigh. "So I'm not sure if I can come and help or not."

Aunt Frances stopped what she was doing and turned around to face Carrie.

"What do you have scheduled?"

"I'm taking tennis, elocution, piano, and a couple of art appreciation workshops. Last week, I nearly forgot the tennis altogether."

Aunt Frances studied Carrie closely, which made Carrie uncomfortable. Aunt Frances could see a lot when she looked right at you. Much more than Mother ever saw.

"And how do you feel about all this?" her aunt asked pointedly.

In spite of herself, Carrie glanced about just to be sure Mother wasn't anywhere near. "I don't really mind the piano lessons."

"What about all the other things?"

Carrie shrugged. "It's all right, I guess. I just wish it weren't during summer." She hesitated to say how much she disliked playing tennis.

Aunt Frances returned to her work, pouring the custard into the ice cream freezer cylinder. "I think this is mostly my fault," she said.

"Your fault? What are you talking about?" The baby had fallen asleep and was a dead weight on Carrie's arm. She turned so her arm was propped against the back of the kitchen chair.

"When your parents came back to Minneapolis from the farm, I dragged your mother off to women's suffrage meetings. I had her involved in every cause and club in the city."

When she finished filling the ice cream freezer, Aunt Frances came over to sit down beside Carrie. "After women got the vote, the rest of us slacked off a little, but not your mama. Now she's just as active in the League of Women Voters as she was in the Suffrage Association. She just doesn't seem to know where or when to stop. And now she's doing the same thing with you."

Carrie knew Aunt Frances was right, but she didn't see what she could do about it.

"Here." Aunt Frances held out her arms to take the sleeping baby. "I'll put him in on the bed. You go tell Larry and Garvey it's time to crush the ice and turn the freezer."

"Yes, ma'am."

As Aunt Frances was leaving the kitchen, she turned and said, "I'll telephone you next week, and we'll see if you can spend an afternoon here with the babies."

"Thanks, Aunt Frances."

Now *that* would be something to look forward to.

CHAPTER 5

The New Girl

The Ruhles' telephone rang at three in the morning on August 3. Father had a telephone by his bed because the news office was liable to call at any hour. Carrie could hear his voice down the hall from her bedroom. Then she heard him talking with Mother.

Carrie lay there listening. When she realized Father was getting dressed, she jumped out of bed and pulled on her housecoat. It must be something truly important for him to be going to the office at this time of night. She stepped into the hallway just as he was coming out of the bedroom.

"What is it, Father?" she asked.

"President Harding. He died last night, and Coolidge has been sworn in. We're going to have to print an extra edition immediately."

"What will that mean—to have a new president?"

Father stopped and put his hand on her shoulder. "Carrie, I'm very sorry that Warren Harding died. But I don't believe this particular change of power is going to affect the nation one way or the other."

He leaned down and kissed her cheek and went on downstairs, stopping at the hall tree to grab his hat.

Crawling back into bed, Carrie couldn't help feeling a little bit important. While the rest of the city slept, she was aware of news that they wouldn't learn until daybreak. It was special to have a newspaperman for a father. Of course, she would never brag about it to anyone, but she lay there and savored the specialness of it.

Later, when she and Mother got up, they listened to the radio. Regular programs were interrupted with the announcement that President Harding had died in San Francisco. The president had been ill for a number of days, but everyone thought he was recovering.

Vice President Calvin Coolidge was vacationing at his boyhood home in Vermont, the announcer explained. "When the vice president was awakened and told the news, his father, John Coolidge, a notary, administered the oath of office by the light of a kerosene lamp."

Listening to the man on the radio, Carrie could picture the scene perfectly. What a surprise that must have been for Mr. Coolidge—to be awakened in the middle of the night and told he was now the president of the United States.

Later that day, as Carrie and Garvey walked to the Simmonses' place to play, Garvey said he'd heard the same announcement. "Uncle Glendon woke us all up at about six," he said. "Then Father gathered us around the radio so we could hear what had happened."

As they walked past the Carrutherses' house, Carrie just happened to look over at the garage apartment. As she did, she thought she saw a face at the window. A girl's face. And she was wearing some kind of scarf. When she looked back again, the face was gone. Could she have been imagining things?

Vi and Nate hadn't heard the news about the president, nor were they much interested. They had other things on their minds.

"You'll never guess what," Vi said as they sat together on the wide porch steps.

"I give up," Garvey said.

"Aunt Oriel has instructed Opal to give us weekly allowances."

"An allowance," Carrie said. "How wonderful." Even though Vi and Nate's aged aunt seldom came out of seclusion, surely she couldn't be all bad. Opal had sometimes given them money out of the grocery fund, but that was every so often—not every week.

"How much?" Garvey wanted to know.

"Twenty cents," Nate told them, holding out his hand to show the four nickels.

Many times Carrie and Garvey had treated the Bickerson children to candy or a movie. But those days were over. Now their friends would have their own money to spend.

"Well, what're we waiting for?" Garvey said, jumping up. "Let's go to the drugstore and get a treat."

As they walked the few blocks to the drugstore, they talked about what they would get. The glass cases in the drugstore were jam-packed with dozens of kinds of candies. It was almost impossible to make a decision. But Carrie knew she didn't want candy on this hot day. She wanted an ice-cold Popsicle.

Once inside the store, Carrie told Mrs. Jenkins, the lady behind the counter, what she wanted. A cloud of cold air was released when Mrs. Jenkins opened the freezer door and handed Carrie the hard, cold, purple Popsicle.

When they came out of the drugstore a few minutes later, Vi had a double-dip chocolate ice-cream cone. The boys had boxes of Cracker Jack, so they could get the toys inside, and chewing gum, so they could get the baseball cards inside.

Carrie nursed her dripping double-stick grape Popsicle. It tasted cold and sweet and yummy. It was so cold it made her teeth ache. They sat down on the curb in front of the drugstore and watched the traffic going by.

As Carrie bit the cold chunks of Popsicle off the sticks, she thought of a poem.

Popsicles, Popsicles—my best pick,
Flavored ice stuck on a stick.
It cools me off in the summer heat;
The yummy flavor is nice and sweet.
Oh, the joy of a Popsicle's hard to beat.

Vi laughed. "I swear, Carrie, you always have a poem going through your head."

"That one would be great for a radio advertisement for Popsicles," Nate said. "If someone put it to music, they could sing it on the air."

"Hey," said Garvey. "What a good idea! I can see it now: Caroline Ruhle, famous radio commercial writer. Let's send it in, Carrie. What do you say?"

Carrie shook her head. "It's not that good," she protested.

Garvey stood up. "Where's that wrapper? Where did you put the wrapper? It'll have the address of the company on it."

"I threw it in the trash inside the drugstore," Carrie said. "Garvey, please. I'm not even sure I could say it again." She often forgot her poems if she didn't write them down as soon as they came to her.

"We'll help you remember," Vi said.

Garvey had already gone inside the drugstore. He came back out carrying the wadded-up wrapper. "The address is right here. Come on. Let's go write it out and send it in."

Carrie ate the last cool bite of Popsicle and threw the sticks in a trash barrel, then hurried to catch up with the other three.

In a matter of minutes, they were under a shade tree in the

Simmonses' backyard. Garvey had a sheet of paper and a pencil in hand. "Now say it again, Carrie," he said. "How did it go?"

Carrie thought a minute. "Popsicles, Popsicles—can't be beat."

"No, no," Vi said. "That's not how it started. It was something about your pick. Rhymed with stick."

"Oh yes. Now I remember." Carrie looked off in the distance to concentrate. Suddenly, at the edge of the Carrutheses' flower garden she saw a little girl. A girl dressed in some kind of foreign peasant garb with a colorful scarf on her head. In a kind of half-whisper, Carrie said, "Look there—by the garden. Who is that?"

The other three looked toward the garden.

"Oh, her," Nate said with a wave of his hand. "Some waif that the chauffeur has taken in. Probably a relative of some sort." Finishing off the last of his Cracker Jack, he added, "Sonny was right when he said Mr. Carruthers shouldn't hire a Jew. Before you know it, there'll be a whole clan of them over there."

"She's trying to catch a kitten," Carrie said.

"That kitten's been roaming around here for days," Vi said. "No one can catch it."

"I bet I could." Carrie watched a minute as the girl slowly tried to inch her way toward the pretty black-and-white kitten. But it let her get only so close and no closer.

"But you're writing a poem about Popsicles, remember?" Nate said firmly.

Carrie wasn't listening. She was walking out of the Simmonses' backyard and over to the Carrutheses' garden. As she approached the girl, she could see she wasn't as young as she'd first thought. The girl was thin, and her face was narrow and pale. From under the scarf, strands of mousy brown hair escaped and floated about her face.

"Hello," Carrie said.

The girl whirled around, her eyes large with fear. She stepped back into the privet hedge as though to hide.

"Don't be afraid," Carrie said gently. "I came to help you with the kitten. Do you speak English?"

At the mention of the kitten, the girl seemed to relax. "I speak some English. It is your kitten?" she asked, pointing to where the little fellow was lying peacefully stretched out in a patch of sunlight.

Carrie shook her head. "The kitten is not mine." Taking another step, she said, "My name is Caroline. My friends all call me Carrie."

"Carrie. Easy to say. Carrie." Placing her thin hand on her chest, the girl said, "Dvora Levinsky."

"Dvora. Is Yerik Levinsky your relative?"

"Relative?" The girl looked puzzled.

"Family. Is he family?"

She nodded and gave a faint smile. "My uncle."

"And the rest of your family?" As soon as she spoke the words, Carrie knew it had been the wrong question.

Dvora pressed her lips tightly together until all the color went out of them. "Sickness on the ship," she said so softly Carrie could barely make out the words. Shaking her head as though to clear out the thoughts, Dvora added, "Mama and Papa, both sick. Both die."

"I'm so very sorry," Carrie said. "How brave you are to come all the way to Minneapolis by yourself."

"I was not brave but very frightened. Only not as frightened as when the Russian peasants burned our village."

Carrie didn't know what to say. Instead, she pointed to the kitten. "Do you want to pet the kitten?"

"Very much I want to, but its feet run too fast."

"Come," Carrie said, motioning toward the walk where the sun streamed down. "Let's sit. We'll let the kitten come to us."

Quietly, gently, so as not to startle the kitten, they sat down together on the walk. "Come, kitty," Carrie said. She tapped the walk with her fingers, making the kitten curious. Presently it stood and stretched, its pink tongue curling up as it made a big yawn. They sat very still as the kitten came and began rubbing against Dvora's funny-looking boots. A smile spread across the girl's face as the kitten crawled right up in her lap.

"It's a girl kitten," Carrie told her.

"Whose kitten could this be?" Dvora asked. Timidly she reached out to touch the furry head. The kitten pushed against her hand, asking for more petting.

"I can find out," Carrie said. "Perhaps she belongs to no one. Perhaps she could be yours."

Dvora looked at Carrie, eyes wide. "How could she be mine?"

"If she belongs to no one, then someone must care for her or she'll die."

The girl nodded, her face serious again. "Yes. Someone must care for her."

"You stay right here. I'll get my friends to help me ask around the neighborhood. We'll soon have an answer."

Carrie stood up slowly so as not to disturb the kitten. Once she got past the garden, she ran back over to the Simmonses' yard, but it was empty. She went in through the kitchen. Opal was there, stirring up something that smelled spicy and good.

"Where is everyone?" Carrie asked.

"Gone to the sandlot."

"Vi, too?"

"Vi, too."

So much for having friends to help. Carrie supposed she'd have to do the asking around the neighborhood all by herself.

CHAPTER 6

Modern Miss Tilden

Carrie wasn't the least bit surprised that no one claimed the kitten. There were stray cats around the city all the time. This would be good news for Dvora. She had to hurry, because it was nearly time for her piano lessons. She couldn't be late this time.

How she wished Vi hadn't gone off with the boys. It was odd for her to do so, because Vi didn't care for baseball any more than Carrie did.

When Carrie returned to the Carrutherses' garden, there was Dvora, still sitting on the walk with the kitten curled up asleep in her lap. Surely her boots, her heavy embroidered dress, and colorful scarf must be awfully warm in the August heat. Dvora, however, seemed oblivious.

"I have good news," Carrie said as she approached. "The kitten is all yours."

She'd no sooner said the words than a man's voice sounded from behind her, startling her. "It was so kind of you to go to the trouble."

She whirled around. There stood Dvora's uncle, the chauffeur, Yerik Levinsky.

Waving his hand toward Dvora, he said, "I asked her to come in out of the hot sun, but she said she wasn't to move."

Carrie's hand flew to her mouth. "Oh dear. I'm afraid that's my fault. I told her to stay right there."

Yerik smiled his nice smile. "She's accustomed to strict obedience." He said something to his niece in strange-sounding words, and Dvora rose, still cradling the docile kitten in her arms.

"Is it all right with you if she keeps the kitten?" Carrie asked. "No one has claimed it."

Yerik nodded. "It is very much all right. At this time, a pet shall be a fine blessing for my niece Dvora."

"I shall name her Vanya." Dvora had stepped up beside them. "It means *gift of God* in Russian."

"A perfect name. Vanya," Carrie repeated. "Tell me, will you be attending school with me in the fall?" she asked.

Dvora glanced at her uncle with questions in her eyes.

"She will," her uncle answered for her. "But I have told her she must cease to wear her babushka before school begins. Giving it up will be difficult for her."

Dvora touched the scarf on her head. That let Carrie know that *babushka* was the name of the unsightly scarf. Her uncle was right—Dvora would most certainly be laughed at if she ever wore such a thing to school.

"I must be going now," Carrie said. "I have to be home in just a few minutes. But I'll see you again soon, I'm sure."

Yerik and Dvora thanked her again for helping with the kitten. She assured them it was no trouble at all. In fact, it had been rather fun.

As Carrie turned to leave, she wished she had time to go to the sandlot and tell Vi all that had happened. But there wasn't a minute to spare.

When she arrived home, Mother was waiting as usual. At least Carrie didn't have to change clothes to go to piano lessons. She ran into the living room to grab her lesson books and sheet music, and off they went.

"I have to run to the department store during your lesson today, Caroline," Mother said as they drove downtown. "Sorry I can't stay and listen."

"That's all right," Carrie said.

It was all right because she'd become used to it. Mother seldom stayed to listen to her lessons.

Carrie's piano teacher, Miss Suzette Tilden, lived in an efficiency apartment not far from the university where she was doing graduate work in music. Miss Tilden was the only single young lady that Carrie knew who rented her very own apartment. Most single women lived at home until they were married. But not Miss Tilden.

Miss Tilden was one of the few women Carrie knew who wore her hair bobbed. That didn't count the movie stars with bobbed hair and pictures in magazines that Carrie had seen. In many ways, Miss Tilden was different than most anyone Carrie knew. The most different thing about her was that she didn't believe in God. Or at least that's what she said.

"God," she had told Carrie many times, "is simply a figment of man's imagination. A figment of the imagination for those who need such a crutch in life."

Carrie wondered how her parents would react if they ever found out about the beliefs of this piano teacher.

Mother slowed the Chandler Six in front of Miss Tilden's apartment building, and Carrie hopped out. "I'll see you in an hour," Mother said and sped off.

"See you in an hour," Carrie said to the exhaust fumes. Then she turned and went up the narrow stairwell that led to the second-floor apartment and tapped at the door.

Miss Tilden called for her to come in. Carrie entered the pint-sized kitchen and made her way through beaded curtains to the living area where the piano was located. Miss Tilden stood from where she'd been sitting at her desk. She read and studied a great deal, and the small apartment was lined with makeshift bookshelves. Magazines lay in stacks on the small tables about the room.

Miss Tilden smiled as she greeted Carrie. Her thin bow-shaped lips were dark with lip rouge. While the rouge was brazen and daring, somehow it looked good on Miss Tilden. It just fit her personality.

"Good afternoon, Miss Tilden," Carrie said, setting her things on the piano. She pulled out the book of Beethoven pieces she'd been working on and set it on the music stand. Although Carrie hated giving up the freedom of summertime hours, she loved the classical music she was studying. Especially Beethoven.

"What would you like to begin with today?" Miss Tilden asked as she joined Carrie at the piano.

Carrie was ashamed that she hadn't practiced well at all the past week. Opening the Beethoven book, she turned to "Moonlight Sonata." It was her favorite. "This one," she said.

When Carrie played it, the song didn't sound nearly as lovely as when she heard it on the radio played by a full orchestra. Slowly, she picked out the melody, stumbling a few times on the left-hand part.

"Pretty good." Miss Tilden set about to drill her on the rough spots, setting the metronome to pace out the rhythm. From there, they moved to Beethoven's famous "Ode to Joy."

"While Beethoven appeared to be a religious man," Miss Tilden said coolly, "we in modern society understand that he was simply clinging to any panacea—any remedy or cure-all—that would comfort him at this time."

"The book says he was totally deaf when he wrote this symphony," Carrie said.

"That's true. And when he wrote many of his other symphonies and an opera."

"But I don't understand, Miss Tilden. I know if I were a musician who had lost my hearing, I would turn to something more than a panacea. I would turn to someone like a loving God who cares about me."

Miss Tilden looked at her for a moment. "If there were a loving God who cares, that loving God would have kept Beethoven from being deaf."

"My aunt Frances says God doesn't stop bad things from happening, but He promises never to leave us. Through the bad times, He's always there."

"That, my dear Carrie, is a highly debatable issue. Now let's stop wasting time talking about the piece. Please play it. All right?"

"Yes, ma'am."

As Carrie played the majestic piece, the words to the hymn taken from its melody ran through her head. They sang it often in church:

Joyful, joyful, we adore Thee, God of glory, Lord of love;
Hearts unfold like flowers before Thee, opening to the sun above.
Melt the clouds of sin and sadness; drive the dark of doubt away;
Giver of immortal gladness, fill us with the light of day!

Perhaps Carrie could pray that God would drive the "dark of doubt" away for Miss Tilden. Carrie couldn't imagine not knowing and loving God. While it was true that her parents didn't pray and read the Bible as much as Aunt Frances and Uncle Kenneth did—nor for that matter, as much as Uncle Hans and Aunt Elena did—they did still took Carrie to church every week.

When the lessons were over, Carrie asked, "Did I tell you that I'm taking tennis lessons this summer, Miss Tilden?"

"I think you mentioned it."

"I'll bet you're a good tennis player."

She nodded as she touched one of the little curls at her cheek. "I can hold my own."

"Why don't you come and play a set or two with me after I take my lesson next week?"

"And where might this be?"

"At the country club."

Miss Tilden gave a bright little laugh. "Sorry, Carrie, I'm not part of the elite class. I wouldn't fit in at your fancy country club."

"You'd be my guest. It's a very nice court. Will you come?"

"I'll think about it and let you know."

"I'll call you the day before to see what you've decided."

"Okay, kiddo. Good enough."

As Carrie tripped down the stairs, she was singing under her breath, "Melt the clouds of sin and sadness; drive the dark of doubt away. . . ."

CHAPTER 7

The Babushka

"Would you drop me off at the sandlot on Franklin Avenue?" Carrie asked Mother on their way home.

"Shouldn't you go home and practice what you learned this afternoon?"

"I promise I'll practice right after supper," Carrie replied.

"All right. But remember, a promise is a promise."

"I'll remember."

Mother slowed the car at the corner vacant lot, where two teams of boys were playing a game of baseball. There was Violet sitting all by herself on the grass under a shade tree. Quickly Carrie kissed her mother good-bye. "I'll just leave my books in the car."

"I'll take them in for you, dear," Mother said.

Carrie jumped out and ran across the lot to where Vi was sitting. Her friend was surrounded by wildflower chains that she'd been weaving. Mostly long-stemmed daisies and brown-eyed Susans.

"Vi," she called out. "Is our team winning?"

Vi looked up, but she didn't smile. "Well, there you are. I thought you'd run off for good. Why didn't you come back?"

"I had to go take my piano lessons."

"No. I mean before that. You stayed with that pitiful Jewish girl for a long time."

"Oh, Vi," Carrie said sitting down. "She really is pitiful. My heart aches for her. Her parents died on the ship coming over. Can you imagine how all alone she must feel?"

Vi proceeded to weave another chain of daisies and said nothing, so Carrie kept talking. "She was entranced with the little kitten. I came to ask the three of you to help me ask around the neighborhood about the kitten, but you'd already left."

"So when you knew I had come to the lot, why didn't you come here?"

Carrie couldn't believe what Vi was saying. "Well, as I was saying—I had to find out if the kitten belonged to anyone."

Vi's voice was cool. "Her uncle could have done that."

"I suppose he could have, but I offered." This was silly. Why was Vi so upset?

"That shows where I rate," Vi said sullenly.

Ignoring the comment, Carrie plunged on. "Anyway, I found out no one had lost a kitten, so I told her it was hers." She paused a minute trying to think of something else to say. "Guess what she named the kitten?"

Vi shrugged, showing she didn't know nor did she care.

"She named it Vanya, which means *gift of God*."

Vi looked up from the daisies in her hand. "What would she know about God?"

Carrie thought a minute, wondering how to answer. She knew so little about Jewish people. "They worship God, Vi."

"Sonny told us that the Jews killed Jesus. You've read the Easter story. You know that's true." Vi shook her head. "I can't believe you'd want to be friends with the very ones who killed Jesus. What kind of Christian are you?"

Carrie stared at her friend. The two of them had been so close for more than a year. Never had one angry word passed between them. Now this. "Dvora is just a little girl, Violet. She's our age. I don't think she had a thing to do with killing Jesus."

Suddenly the winning home run went sailing over their heads, bringing their conversation to a halt. The game was over, and the boys were whooping and hollering something fierce. The girls couldn't have continued their conversation if they'd wanted to. And Carrie definitely didn't want to.

The four of them went trooping back to the Simmonses' house for lemonade and cookies that Opal had prepared. The boys could talk of nothing but the wonderful plays they'd made and the home runs they'd hit. Thankfully, Vi didn't bring up the subject of Dvora.

Carrie relished the long, hot days of summer, but school was looming just around the corner. Every time she passed the Carrutherses' place to go play with Violet and Nate, she wondered if Dvora had yet given up her babushka. But then she would see the girl either sitting at the window in the apartment or sitting on the steps with the kitten in her lap. And without fail, the babushka would still be tied on her head.

One afternoon, Nate and Garvey were off playing ball again, and Vi and Carrie had played together in the attic for hours. When it was time for Carrie to go home, she was by herself walking past the Carrutherses' house. Yerik was out front in the circle driveway polishing the Packard.

"Excuse me, Miss Caroline," he said as she approached. "Could you spare a minute?"

His voice startled her. She hadn't expected him to speak to her. "I have a few minutes," she answered.

He shook his head. "About Dvora," he said.

"Is she ill?" Carrie asked. The girl had seemed as frail as a china doll.

"No. Not in body at least." Yerik folded the polishing cloth in his hands. "I'm a bachelor man, not a father. I know so little about young girls."

Carrie could see how that might be a problem.

"It's about the babushka."

"Oh," Carrie said, now understanding the problem.

"You see, Miss Caroline, the babushka belonged to Dvora's sweet mother—my sister, Chava. And before Chava, it belonged to our mother—Chava's and mine." There were tears in Yerik's eyes, but Carrie was polite and pretended not to notice.

"On the ship, before Chava died, she used her last remaining strength to remove the babushka from her own head and place it over Dvora's." Yerik swallowed hard and continued to fold and unfold the polishing cloth. "It is the only article my niece has of her mama's. This is why she refuses to take it off."

The story was sad enough to make Carrie cry, and she hadn't even known this Jewish mother who died out on the ocean some-where. "Why are you telling me this?" Carrie asked. She was sup-posed to be home for supper in just a few minutes.

"I am presuming too much to speak to you of this." His eyes turned shyly to the pavement at his feet. "Yet I thought because of your kindness with the kitten, that perhaps you might talk to her of the babushka."

Carrie hesitated for a moment. "I suppose I could take just a minute with her." This was silly, because she had no earthly idea what she could say that would make any difference.

"Come, I'll show you to the apartment."

"I know the way. Shall I just knock?"

"Yes, just knock."

As Carrie walked around the house to the garage, it occurred to her to say a quick prayer. After all, God knew how Dvora's heart was broken at losing her parents.

The Levinskys' apartment was furnished quite simply and was scrubbed as spotless as Aunt Frances's house. Dvora greeted Carrie warmly. "Welcome to our house, Carrie," she said. "Come and sit with me." She waved toward a small wooden kitchen table. She fixed strong tea in glasses with no ice.

She showed Carrie the box that was supposed to be the kitten's bed. "But," she said, "mostly Vanya wants to sleep with me."

"That means she loves you."

Dvora gave a shy smile. "I think she does."

"Before school begins," Carrie said, "I'd like to help you fix your hair. May I do that?"

Dvora's hand flew to her braid, which was entwined with a bright red ribbon and coiled around her head—all covered, of course, with the scarf. "My hair is not right?"

"Your hair is very pretty, but I can help you make it look more American."

Dvora pointed to Carrie's long braids. "Down like yours?"

Carrie nodded. "May I try? Not today, but another day?"

"But the babushka. . . ," Dvora said, her eyes getting all misty. She toyed with the tie beneath her chin.

"The cloth is beautiful. Was it woven by your family?"

Dvora nodded. "Woven many generations ago."

"Could you show me more closely?" Carrie asked carefully. "Could we spread it out on the table?"

"Yes. You will better see how lovely it is." With that, Dvora untied the scarf and spread it out across the table.

Carrie admired the intricacies of the weave and the delicate floral pattern. "It would make a lovely sash."

"A sash?"

"Worn at the waist." Gently she took the cloth, folded it, and put it around Dvora's waist.

"Girls at your school wear a sash?"

Carrie nodded. "They do."

"They don't wear babushkas?" Dvora pointed to her head.

"No, Dvora. No one at Washington Elementary School wears a babushka." Carrie took the cloth and folded it loosely about Dvora's neck. "It could even be a scarf at the neck."

Dvora nodded and smiled. "I can see that it might be a scarf at the neck." She took the babushka from Carrie's hands and tied a little knot at her neck. "Uncle Yerik is taking me to purchase shoes and school dresses tomorrow."

"Good," Carrie said. "That's good. The salesladies at the stores will help you make the right choices." Carrie rose to go. "I'll help you with your hair on another day."

"Thank you, Carrie. Again you have been a friend to me."

As Carrie hurried out the drive, she hoped against hope that Violet wasn't looking out of her window.

A welcome gray thunderstorm moved across the city the week before school began, settling the dust and cooling the terribly hot temperatures. And it provided Carrie and Garvey and the Bickersons with another wonderful day to play in the attic.

This time, Garvey had his head wound up in a turban, which made him look ridiculous. "I'm Rudolph Valentino," he said, throwing a tablecloth about his shoulders for a cape. "I'm the sheik."

Vi laughed at his antics. "You don't look anything like Rudolph Valentino," she protested. "Rudolph is handsome. His eyes are sultry, and his hair is slicked back all shiny with nothing out of place."

"Well, this is just pretend anyway," Garvey said, laughing. As he whirled his cape, the turban unwound and fell to his feet.

"I'd rather be Douglas Fairbanks playing Robin Hood," Nate said.

"That would be fun," Vi agreed. "And I could be Maid Marian."

Garvey, picking up a cane and holding it like a staff, was now ready for the new game. "I, of course, will be the biggest and strongest one of his merry men—Little John."

"Who will I be?" Carrie wanted to know.

"Why, my lady-in-waiting, of course," Violet replied.

Although Carrie felt she'd been a trifle cheated, still they had fun with the game for several hours. The rain continued to beat down on the attic windows as they played. Even when Garvey got a little overly enthusiastic with his staff and accidentally hit Nate in the head, no one got upset.

Then Nate happened to remember something. "Garvey, guess what? The Yankees are playing this afternoon. Why don't we go to your house and listen to the game on the radio? Wouldn't it be great to hear the Babe slug a couple of homers?"

"I have a better idea," Garvey said, removing his pretend cape. "Sonny's gone to work for the day. Let's just go down and listen on his radio set."

"What a great idea," Nate said.

"He'll kill you if he finds out," Vi said. But Carrie could tell she was just as excited about the idea as the boys were.

"He won't find out," Garvey said. "We're not going to hurt anything. All we'll do is turn the set on, tune it in, then turn it back off again."

Vi was already pulling off her long dress-up dress. "Come on," she said to Carrie. "This'll be great fun."

Carrie didn't think it would be great fun at all. But she said nothing. Reluctantly she folded up her old dress, placed it back in the trunk, and followed the trio down the stairs.

CHAPTER 8

Secret in the Closet

"We'll act like we're going outside," Garvey said quietly. "Then we'll enter from the outside entrance. That way Opal won't get suspicious."

"Keen idea," Nate said, really getting into the drama of the escapade.

Carrie couldn't see any fun in sneaking around and snooping into another person's belongings. But she said nothing.

"I get to turn it on," Nate said as they came down the steps from the outside entrance and quietly entered the room where the radio set was kept.

"Then I'll tune it in," Garvey said. "I'm used to doing that with our set at home."

Carrie wondered if Garvey remembered that her family purchased a radio months before his family had, and her father had allowed her to tune it in the very first day it arrived. There was really nothing to it, but Garvey made it sound as though it required special ability.

The four walked over to the workbench where the radio was sitting. The place was littered with wires and tubes and gadgets of all kinds. Wiring charts were posted on the wall above the radio, and books about radio sets were lined in a row against the back wall. Sonny now worked at a radio shop downtown. It was obvious he was quite taken with radios.

Garvey studied the titles of the books. "I bet these books are hard to understand," he said. "I'm doing well to get through a couple episodes of *The Radio Boys*."

Once the game was tuned in, Carrie wondered how long it would be before Vi became bored with listening. After all, Vi had always said that watching a ball game was boring. Listening was even more so.

"Let's sit down over here," Vi said, her eyes sparkling with the excitement of it all. She seated herself on a chenille rug and waved to Carrie to join her.

Although it didn't look any too clean, Carrie supposed the rug couldn't be any dustier than the attic. She sat down and prepared to endure.

At home, if Father listened to a game, Carrie could go off and play by herself or read in her room. But now she listened as the fast-talking announcer described play after play that meant nothing to Carrie.

"Shh!" Garvey said at one point, even though no one was talking. "The Bambino is at bat."

"Come on, Number Three," Nate said, referring to Babe Ruth's uniform number.

When the homer was slammed, Garvey, who was leaning close to the radio, jumped for joy. As he did, his arm accidentally knocked two glass radio tubes to the floor. One bounced. The other shattered.

All four friends were silent for a moment as the announcer continued the play-by-play, accompanied by sounds of cheering crowds in the background.

"Aw, Garvey," Nate said. "What'd you have to go and do that for?"

"Hey, I didn't mean to."

"You should have stayed back a ways," Vi scolded.

"I had to stay close to keep it tuned in."

"Now we'll have to go buy another tube," Nate said.

"And fast, too," Carrie reminded them, "before Sonny gets home."

Garvey reached into his pocket. "We're all in this together. Let's pool our money for the new tube."

Nate groaned as he dug in his pockets. Among the four of them, they had ninety-five cents, fifty of which came from Carrie. That certainly wasn't how she'd planned to spend her extra money.

"You girls sweep up the glass," Garvey instructed, "and we'll be back with a new tube in a few minutes."

As soon as the boys were gone, Vi looked around the room. "Where do you suppose Sonny would keep a broom and dustpan?" she asked.

"I don't know. Doesn't look like he uses a broom very often."

Vi ignored the comment as she continued peeking into corners and opening doors.

Carrie went toward the stairs that led up to the back hallway. She thought there might be a closet under the stairs, and she was right. Opening the door, she reached up to pull a light chain. The bulb illuminated a small closet full of cleaning supplies. Opal probably kept extra things down there so she wouldn't have to tote them up and down the stairs.

As Carrie reached for the broom, she noticed something lying in the corner. Something white. She froze where she stood. "Vi," she said softly. "Come here."

"What is it? Did you find a broom?"

"Yes. And something else."

Vi peered around the door frame. "What? I don't see anything."

64

"In the corner." Carrie stepped out of the way.

"It looks like an old sheet to me." Then Vi drew in her breath. "Oh my goodness. Is that what I think it is?" She knelt down and gently picked up the corner of the cloth. Out fell a hood with the eyes cut out. Vi looked up at Carrie, her eyes wide. "Sonny's a member of the Klan," she said in a frightened whisper.

Carrie had heard her father talk a great deal about the horrors of the Ku Klux Klan. He never had a good word to say about their scare tactics and their hatred for people of other races and faiths. She thought of Dvora and Yerik next door, and she shivered.

"I knew Sonny had been keeping some pretty late hours," Vi said. "Now I know why." Refolding the robe and hood, she said, "Let's hurry and get the glass swept up. We'll tell the boys about this when they get back."

The new radio tube cost eighty-nine cents, which made Carrie thankful she didn't buy those kinds of things every day. A Popsicle and a movie were much cheaper.

Nate gave the six-cents change back to Carrie since she'd contributed the most toward the new tube. The broken glass was put in a paper bag to be disposed of in the garbage can in the back of the house. But first, the girls took Nate and Garvey back to the closet to show them the robe and hood.

Carrie could tell Garvey was trying hard to mask his shock. He grabbed the hood and pulled it over his head. "Look at me," he said in a silly tone. "I'm in the Klan!" Pulling it off again, he added, "Too bad we don't have this up in the attic. What a great game that would be."

"Garvey," she scolded, "that's not very funny."

"Oh, you're just an old stick-in-the-mud," Garvey spouted back to her.

Nate was more cool about the discovery. Perhaps he'd known all along. "So what's the big uproar?" he said, directing his attention to his sister. "Sonny's almost eighteen. I guess he can do whatever he wants to, can't he?"

"But the Klan. . . ," Vi countered. "He may have helped burn crosses in the yard of some black person—or at the home of a family of Catholics."

"Burning crosses never hurt anyone," Nate snapped.

Carrie glanced at Violet. Her friend gave a shrug.

"I'd better get on home," Carrie said.

"The rain's let up," Garvey said, elbowing Nate in the ribs as though to knock him out of his serious mood. "Let's go see if anyone wants to play ball."

On her way home, Carrie thought about the Klan robe. She'd seen photos of Klan marches in the newspapers. It was eerie to think that she personally knew someone who was hiding under one of those crazy getups.

When she got home, she went to her room and wrote a new poem in her poetry notebook:

Evil deeds avoid the light.
Evil men ignore what's right.
Klansmen feed on fear and hate.
Hurrying to mischief, they cannot wait.

CHAPTER 9

Country Club Encounter

On the first day of school, Dvora looked very nice in her blue linen dress with the babushka draped like a sash at her waist. Her braids hung down her back rather than wound around her head, just as Carrie had shown her. Dvora had been attending English classes with other Jewish children whenever Yerik could take her. But her uncle had very few free hours, so the lessons were limited.

While she looked much like all the other children on the playground, it was when Dvora opened her mouth to speak that the truth came spilling out. Her broken English was difficult to understand. Not that she spoke much. In fact, during the first few days of school, she seldom talked to anyone.

There were other immigrant children at Washington Elementary that fall. Nearly all of them were ignored just as Dvora was. But Carrie didn't know the other immigrant children. She knew Dvora, and her heart broke for her. How strange the schoolroom must look to this girl so new in this country. A girl who had been accustomed to a tiny cottage in a small village, surrounded by farmland. Dvora didn't even know what chalk was. Nor Crayolas. Carrie longed to reach out and help the Jewish girl. But she also wanted to keep her friendship with Vi.

Vi and Garvey were with Carrie in the fifth-grade classroom. Nate was in sixth grade. Carrie had looked forward to this year because Mrs. Harwell was known all through the school for her unique nature and science projects.

Potted plants perched on nearly every windowsill—from ferns, to cacti, to African violets. A large terrarium held a garter snake, a frog, and a lizard.

Outside the window, the teacher had rigged up a bird-feeding station. The students were assigned to take turns putting out the feed each day. A bird book was kept on a table near the window, and a notebook where they could chart which birds came to feed was also kept there.

Carrie immediately liked Mrs. Harwell. She took special note of how kind this teacher was to the immigrant children, including Dvora.

Recess time at Washington Elementary meant baseball games. Nearly every boy wanted to be included. Sometimes they played one grade against another. Other times, they voted captains and chose up sides. Baseball cards were in their pockets, and scores and statistics were spoken with great accuracy. Heated arguments could be heard over whether the Giants or the Yankees were the best team. Nate and Garvey were always for the Yankees—mainly because that was the Babe's team. At times, Carrie wondered how the boys could ever study because their brains were so filled up with baseball.

Convincing her piano teacher to come to the country club to play a game of tennis had been more difficult than Carrie had first thought it would be. Miss Tilden continued to give feeble excuses. Carrie suspected if she were taking lessons any place other than the country club, Miss Tilden might have accepted right off.

Her tennis lessons were now after school on Thursday afternoons. That meant she had to hurry home from school and change into her tennis togs so Mother could drive her out to the club.

One afternoon as she was finishing up a lesson, Carrie hung back, helping Mr. Clausen pick up all the balls and put them in the wicker basket at the side of the court.

"Thanks for your help, Carrie," he said. "Shouldn't you be going? Isn't your mother out there waiting on you?"

"She won't leave without me," Carrie answered absently. She had a question to ask, but she had no idea how to begin.

Mr. Clausen stopped a moment, wiping his forehead with the white towel slung about his neck. He still held his wonderful summer tan, and his blue eyes were positively electric. "Is there something on your mind, Carrie?"

"Well, yes. Now that you ask."

"About tennis?"

"No," she said, smiling. "Never about tennis."

"I thought not. Then what is it?"

"You're going to be a pastor someday. What would you say to someone who said to you that they hated Jews because the Jews killed Jesus? What would you say to such a thing?"

Mr. Clausen's handsome face grew serious. "That's a very important question, Carrie. I've certainly heard that said from time to time. Usually it's said by someone who is looking for reasons to hate or dislike someone."

Carrie thought of Sonny and nodded.

"The truth of the matter is, each one of us killed Jesus. He died for the sins of every man and woman, every girl and boy. He bore our sins for us, so it was our sins that killed Him." He paused and looked at her a moment. "Does that make sense, Carrie?"

"I think so."

"Of course, we know from reading the Gospels that a group of Jews and Romans plotted together to do the actual killing. But don't forget there were hundreds of Jews at the same time who followed Jesus, who believed in Him, and who loved Him very much. We know that's true, don't we?"

Carrie gave a vigorous nod.

"In fact, it was that handful of Jewish followers who started the church after Jesus' resurrection." He put his arm on her shoulder to steer her toward the clubhouse. "It was God's choice to have Jesus born into the Jewish bloodline. In my opinion, that means I owe a great deal to the Jews. God called them His chosen people. I can do no less."

"Wow, Mr. Clausen. I never thought of that."

"Does that answer your question?"

"It sure does." Carrie suddenly felt much less bothered by Vi's question.

"Any more questions?"

"Just one. My piano teacher doesn't believe in God. If I invited her to come and play tennis with me, would you talk to her?"

"Your piano teacher?"

"Yes, sir."

"Can she play tennis?"

Carrie tried to remember what Suzette Tilden had said about tennis. "Some, I think."

He nodded and smiled. "Why, sure. If you get her here, I'll talk to her."

"Thanks, Mr. Clausen." Carrie really did have to hurry then. She could see Mother standing at the clubhouse door with her arms folded and looking horribly impatient.

Two weeks later, Carrie was just finishing her piano lesson at Miss Tilden's apartment. For the umpteenth time, she invited her teacher to come play a game of tennis with her.

"It doesn't matter if you're not very good," Carrie said, "because I'm not very good, either."

"You never give up, do you? Oh, all right, Carrie. When shall I come?"

Carrie was suddenly so excited she could hardly think. But she was able to set a time following her tennis lesson and give directions to the tennis courts. "If anyone stops you, just say you're a guest of Nolan Clausen. He's my instructor."

"Nolan Clausen." Miss Tilden scribbled the name on a notepad. "All right, Carrie," she said as she ushered Carrie out the door. "I'll see you and the elite country club tomorrow afternoon."

The next step in Carrie's plan was to ask Mother to play a game of doubles following her tennis lesson. That was almost as difficult as getting Miss Tilden to the courts in the first place. "You've paid all this money," went her argument. "Wouldn't you like to see how I'm doing?" Then she added, "Think how much fun we'd have."

Finally, her mother said yes, as well.

All day at school on Thursday, Carrie was nervously thinking about the get-together that afternoon. She was sure Mr. Clausen could help Miss Tilden understand about God and to come to know how much He loves everyone.

The day was unusually warm for late September, and the sun was shining. All during her lesson, Carrie was in her worst form ever. She never was very good, but on this day, she played horribly.

Mr. Clausen never got upset with her. In fact, he was smiling. "You seem to have your mind in other places today, Carrie," he said.

"I suppose I do," she admitted.

Just then, a voice from behind her called her name. She whirled around to see Miss Tilden looking chic in her pleated skirt, trim middy blouse, and neat little canvas shoes with turned-down cotton socks. On her bobbed hair sat a jaunty beret. Her lips were rouged even more than usual.

"Miss Tilden! There you are," Carrie exclaimed.

When Carrie introduced the two, Miss Tilden gave Mr. Clausen her loveliest smile. They shook hands and were quickly calling one another *Suzette* and *Nolan*.

At just the right moment, Mother arrived dressed and ready to play. Since Mother knew the two instructors, there was no need for further introductions. Mr. Clausen suggested he and Miss Tilden play mother and daughter. But Miss Tilden said she didn't think that would be very fair.

"I'll team with Mrs. Ruhle," she said, "and you be a support to your student here."

Mr. Clausen smiled and nodded. After the first set, Carrie realized what Miss Tilden meant. She was a much better player than she'd let on.

At first, Mr. Clausen was playing to humor Miss Tilden and to make things easy for her. That ended quickly. Carrie laughed to see how much dancing around Mr. Clausen had to do just to keep up with Miss Tilden's expertly placed lobs and backhands. She kept him on his heels quite a bit.

With Mr. Clausen beside her, Carrie felt more confident than she ever had. Suddenly, in a real, honest-to-goodness game, all his instructions came home to her, and she rose to the occasion. And

72

Mother's game wasn't anything to complain about. In the end, there was fierce competition and some hard playing—Mother and Miss Tilden won two sets to Mr. Clausen and Carrie's one.

In the midst of the laughing and shaking of hands at the end of their matches, Mr. Clausen suggested they all have something cold to drink before leaving. Carrie was hoping he'd say such a thing. She also hoped Mother would say yes, and she did.

The three adults were complimenting Carrie on her game, which made her feel terrific. They sat around one of the patio tables, enjoying the cool breeze that had come up. Small talk followed as they sipped their iced drinks.

Presently Carrie said to Miss Tilden, "Mr. Clausen here is still in school, just like you are."

"Oh, really?" She looked over at the tennis instructor, her plucked brows raised. "Studying what?"

"He's in divinity school," Carrie informed her. "Someday he'll be a pastor."

As soon as she said those words, a mask fell over Miss Tilden's face. Her rouged lips pursed together in a frown.

Carrie quickly plunged on. "One day, he'll be preaching in the pulpit telling people all about God's love and mercy. Won't you, Mr. Clausen?"

Mr. Clausen, too, had caught Miss Tilden's sudden reaction. "That's right, Carrie."

"Fleecing the sheep," Miss Tilden said, her voice suddenly cool and aloof. "Isn't that an apt description for most so-called preachers? Standing up there looking holy, telling people how to live, yet never quite making it themselves. Telling the people to give to the church so they can pay the rent."

Mother straightened her back. "Pardon me, Suzette, but that's not at all what a pastor does. Of course, no one is perfect, but the pastor's job is to point us to God and to God's Word. While Jesus is our true Shepherd, our pastors are the 'undershepherds.' "

Carrie listened in amazement as her mother gently continued. "I've gone to church nearly all my life. Through those years, God's Word and God's people have always been a source of comfort and strength to me."

The words surprised Carrie. She hadn't heard Mother talk like that for a very long time.

Suddenly, Miss Tilden's chair scooted noisily against the flagstones. "So," she blurted out to Carrie, "is this why you've plotted and planned to corner me here? Has your little scheme worked? Did you think if I were talked to by a good-looking man that I'd be suddenly converted?"

"Oh, no—" Carrie started.

But Miss Tilden was not listening. She stood up. "Well, let me tell you, better people than you have tried and failed. Just consider that this is one fish that got away. I'm not jumping to any hook, no matter how good the bait looks."

With that, she stomped across the patio and into the clubhouse.

Carrie felt as though she wanted to wither up and die.

Mr. Clausen reached over and patted her hand. "Don't fret, Carrie," he told her. "Your heart was in the right place. Just keep praying. I don't think Suzette is nearly as tough as she appears."

The words were no encouragement at all. Carrie didn't know how she would face her piano teacher ever again.

CHAPTER 10

World Series

"The Babe's the greatest!" Garvey stood with his hands on his hips and a scowl on his face. He was on the schoolgrounds, facing off with another fifth-grader named Wally.

"He is not," Wally spouted back. "He's a has-been. My uncle lives in New York. Goes to see him play right there in the brand-spanking-new Yankee Stadium. He says the Babe doesn't train properly, and he's getting too old. He's all washed up."

"That's a bunch of hogwash," Garvey retorted. "What does your uncle know, anyhow? How can you call forty-one home runs being washed up?"

"He's almost twenty-nine years old," Wally flailed back, now almost nose-to-nose with Garvey. "That's too old to be playing ball."

"For other men, maybe," Garvey conceded. "But not for the Babe. He's bigger and better than all the rest."

Carrie and Violet were sitting on the jungle gym, listening to the feud, a feud that seemed to go on endlessly now that the World Series was only a week away. That morning, in the first hour, Mrs. Harwell had announced that the ladies who worked in the school office planned to keep the radio on during the Series. They promised to report the scores at the end of each inning. Every boy in fifth grade cheered the announcement.

Even though Carrie wasn't much interested in baseball, she tended to agree with Garvey. She'd often seen Babe Ruth in the newsreels. He seemed like a magical person. Bigger and more famous even than all the movie stars. He was flocked by children wherever he went, and he never turned them away. The newsreels showed him visiting orphanages and hospitals, where he took time to autograph baseballs and give them to the children. It was no wonder Garvey and Nate worshiped him so.

Garvey and Wally's standoff never came to blows. They seldom did. Before recess was over, they were playing ball together once again.

That afternoon, Garvey slipped up to Wally and apologized for being so harsh with him earlier. Wally smiled and accepted the apology. What he didn't know was that in his other hand, Garvey had a sign and a piece of adhesive tape. When he walked away, a sign was stuck to Wally's back that announced to the world: "THE BABE'S THE GREATEST!"

Carrie was terribly concerned about Dvora's schoolwork. The new girl tried hard, but Carrie could see there were concepts in math and science that Dvora wasn't catching. How she wished there were some way she could help. But how?

The day Dvora appeared to be the happiest was when it came her turn to work at the window with the birds. Mrs. Harwell kept a list of whose turn came on which days, and she was kind enough to team Carrie and Dvora together. Dvora was to put out the feed, and Carrie logged in the book the names and numbers of the birds that came to the feeder during a span of two hours. The fall breeze coming in the open window felt crisp and clean.

"So many different kinds of birds God made," Dvora said as she poured seed out on the feeding station. "He makes all kinds and all sizes, just like people."

Carrie smiled. "That's true, Dvora. All kinds and all sizes."

Dvora closed the window and watched for a minute as the birds came flocking in. They knew right where their breakfast was located. Carrie noted the finches and the chickadees, the blue jays and starlings, marking them down in the proper place in the notebook. While she enjoyed watching the birds come in to feed, she enjoyed the smile on Dvora's face even more.

Mrs. Harwell had a difficult time teaching anything of any substance during the World Series. The first game came on Wednesday, October 10, and as promised, the ladies who worked in the office came to the classes at the end of each inning to announce the scores. The announcements were accompanied by cheers or moans, depending on who was ahead.

It wasn't the World Series that was on Carrie's mind that week. She was worrying herself half sick, wondering what would happen at her next piano lesson. Miss Tilden, no doubt, was furious with her.

In spite of a nippy October wind, Carrie's hand was sweaty as she turned the knob leading to the narrow stairway. Standing inside on the bottom landing, she shifted the books in her arms, then wiped her sweaty hand on her coat. She stood there a moment, waiting for the nervousness to go away. But then she realized Miss Tilden had surely heard the door open. How silly it was for her to just stand there like a dunderhead. After all, if she'd had the courage to ask Miss Tilden to come to the country club in the first place, why wouldn't she have the courage to face her now?

This thought moved Carrie slowly up the stairs. Softly, she knocked and heard her teacher's voice inviting her to come in. Her Mary Jane patent leather shoes squeaked loudly on the kitchen linoleum. The strings of beads hanging at the kitchen door clattered more than they ever had before. Miss Tilden was sitting at her desk. She didn't look up.

"Make yourself comfortable, Caroline. Be with you shortly."

"Yes, ma'am."

Carrie removed her coat and hung it across the back of a chair, took out her music and placed it on the piano, then waited. She needed a drink of water for her dry throat, but she didn't want to ask.

Miss Tilden shuffled a few papers on her desk. The desk drawer opened and closed with a screaky noise. She rose and came to the piano. "Did you practice your lessons this week?" she asked.

"Yes, ma'am," Carrie replied as well as she could around her dry throat.

"Good. Let's get started then."

And that was it. All Carrie's worrying had been for nothing. While Miss Tilden was cool and reserved, the subject of the tennis match was never mentioned. Carrie never expected this. She thought surely Miss Tilden was going to accuse her of all sorts of terrible things. But to have her avoid talking about it altogether took Carrie off guard.

Throughout the lesson, Carrie kept wondering if she should bring up the subject. Should she apologize? But if she apologized, what would she apologize for? She was still very pleased that Miss Tilden and Mr. Clausen met. And she was glad they all had such a good time together. Of course, she was sorry that Miss Tilden had gotten so upset, but that wasn't Carrie's fault. Miss Tilden got upset on her own.

Carrie could honestly say she wasn't sorry for planning the whole thing. But now, to have Miss Tilden be so cool. . . Well, it was all too, too confusing.

In spite of everything, the lines of the hymn kept running through her mind: *Melt the clouds of sin and sadness; drive the dark of doubt away. . . .* That's what she prayed for her piano teacher.

Nate spent Saturday at Garvey's house so they could listen to the fourth game of the World Series on the Constables' radio. Carrie took some of her dolls and went to play with Vi for the day. They played house in the attic for a time, but since it was such a sunny day, they also played jacks in front of the house.

Carrie kept glancing over to the garage where Dvora lived, wondering how she was doing. Vi noticed her looking in that direction and said, "She never comes outside on Saturdays. Never."

"That's because Saturday is their Sabbath."

"What does that mean?" Vi asked.

"It just means they worship on Saturday like we worship on Sunday. Sort of."

"Sort of?"

"All I know is they light candles and eat braided bread called *challah*. And they do no work, and they don't go anyplace."

Vi threw out the jacks, bounced the ball, and began picking up the jacks between bounces. "I think I like our Sundays better. Before Mother and Father died, we used to always go for a drive on Sunday afternoons. It didn't matter that we traveled on Sundays."

Late in the afternoon, they were in Vi's bedroom, sitting on her bed and looking at copies of *Moving Picture* magazine. The stars wore such elegant clothes—dresses and outfits that must cost thousands of dollars. This turned the girls' conversation to what girls were wearing to school that year.

"I may not have the fanciest clothes at Washington Elementary," Vi said, "but at least I don't wear the same silly sash day after day like that Dvora girl does." Vi wrinkled her freckled nose. "If she isn't wearing it at her waist, she's got it around her shoulders. It's almost like a baby carrying a special blanket around."

"Vi, don't say that. It is very special to her and wearing it does comfort her."

Vi's green eyes narrowed. "Why are you always defending her? No matter what I say, you always defend the Jewish girl."

"I don't always defend her," Carrie said, "but someone should. She's never hurt anyone."

"Sonny says the Jews have all the money in America and that they're very dangerous."

Carrie shook her head. "Remember who Sonny has been listening to. Those Klan members would say anything to stir up hatred."

"Maybe in some things the Klan members are right," Vi said.

Carrie was quiet. She didn't think for a minute that her friend really meant those words. "Oh, Vi," she said, "this is silly. We start talking about movie stars and school clothes and wind up talking about the Ku Klux Klan—something we don't know a thing about." She put down the magazine, jumped up from the bed, and said, "Come on, Vi. I bet Opal's got some special treat for us in the kitchen. I'm starved, aren't you?"

To Carrie's great relief, that ended the conversation about poor Dvora. But that night as she lay in bed, she wooled it over in her mind. Why didn't Violet like Dvora? How she wished the three of them could be friends. As she drifted off to sleep, a poem floated through her mind:

People fear what they do not know.
How I wish it were not so.
Suzette's afraid of a God who gives love.
Vi's afraid of a girl who needs love.

On Sunday afternoon, Nate was included in the weekly family gathering at the Constables'. After all, as Garvey explained it, to deprive him of listening to the fifth game of the World Series would have been cruel and unusual punishment.

The usual conversation was nonexistent as the radio blared out the plays. The men—and the boys—alternately cheered and booed. The women felt rather dispossessed. If the men had been in the middle of a conversation, they would have joined in. But this. . . this ball game business. This was different.

Out in the kitchen, Aunt Frances shook her head in dismay. "I never thought I'd see the day when my own family would be sitting around on a Sunday afternoon listening to a baseball game," she said. "Why, our parents would be in a state of shock if they ever saw such a thing."

Even as she said the words, the Babe had slammed another homer with the announcer describing his dramatic trot around the bases. "And now, fans," the announcer continued, "the Bambino is on his feet, doffing his hat to the crowds here in Yankee Stadium. And the crowd is going wild."

And so were the men in the Constables' front room. There was no doubt the Yankees had the 1923 World Series in their pocket. Everyone in the Constable household seemed to be happy about it. The best part, in Carrie's opinion, was that there was now only one game left to play.

The women joined the men after the game was over, and music

again came over the speaker of the radio console. Normal conversation returned. Uncle Ken took the opportunity to ask Father if he still planned to go to Detroit to see the radio station.

"I almost have my boss convinced," Father replied with a smile. Turning to Larry, he added, "Look for a pilot with a trustworthy plane. I may be needing it."

"I have just the one for you," Larry replied.

Carrie thought it would be terribly exciting if Father were able to take a plane ride all the way to Detroit. She would want to hear every exciting detail when he returned.

CHAPTER 11

Dvora's Story

"I want to help tutor Dvora Levinsky a couple afternoons a week after school." Carrie made this bold announcement to her parents at supper one evening. She'd been thinking and thinking about how to help the girl. Dvora was unable to grasp the lessons, and it was so sad to watch her fail. Finally Carrie could stand it no longer. She had to do something.

Mother's first response was, "What about your tennis lessons? Your piano lessons? Your elocution lessons?"

Father wanted to know, "Did your teacher ask you to do this? How do you know anything about tutoring?"

"I may not know much about tutoring, but Dvora trusts me. I think we would work well together. And no, my teacher didn't ask me. In fact, I haven't asked her for permission yet."

"And what makes you think she will agree?" Father asked.

Carrie smiled. "Because I know Mrs. Harwell." Then to her mother, she said, "I think I've learned enough tennis to get me through life in good order. And if we left off the elocution lessons, I could pick them back up later, after Dvora is over this hump. I would like to continue my music though," she added.

Carrie wanted very much to keep in contact with Miss Tilden, but she didn't say that.

Father leaned back in his chair and thought for a moment.

"What do you think, Glendon?" Mother asked. "Is it safe for her to spend that much time with a foreigner?"

Father gave a little laugh. "I don't think it will hurt her at all, Ida," he replied. "Here we are, you and I, always absorbed in issues of public interest. What is it you always say? 'We must give back to society and not always take.' Now our daughter is doing exactly that. Should we be surprised? I say let her reach out and help this girl. We'll all be the better for it."

Carrie jumped up from her chair and ran to hug her father's neck. "Oh, thank you, Father. This will be such good news for Dvora."

Mother exhaled a deep sigh and folded her napkin. "I'll telephone the country club tomorrow to cancel the lessons," she said, with a tone of reluctance in her voice. "And your elocution teacher, as well."

Carrie was right about two things. Mrs. Harwell was all in favor of her helping Dvora with her studies. And Dvora was happier than Carrie had ever seen her. They settled on two afternoons a week.

The missing piece to the puzzle was how Vi would react. Carrie found out soon enough. "You're a traitor to your friends and your school," Vi said through clenched teeth. "I can't believe you would ever do such a thing."

Then Carrie realized it wasn't only Vi's reaction she had to be concerned about. Nate didn't much like the idea either. "It's best to leave 'those kind' to themselves," he said, his voice heavy with bitterness.

That, in turn, made Garvey upset. "We were all four getting along just fine until the little peasant girl moved in above the garage," he said to Carrie. "Why couldn't you just leave well enough alone?"

Carrie could hardly believe this was her cousin talking—Garvey Constable, who was more like a brother to her than a cousin. The whole thing was like an ugly snowball that kept on growing.

One day in private, Mrs. Harwell said to Carrie, "I know your good deeds toward Dvora are not making you the most popular girl in the fifth grade, but don't give up. It will be worth it all. You'll see."

But the hours spent with Dvora in the Levinskys' small clean kitchen were delightful. As they studied, the two girls could hear Dvora's uncle Yerik below them tinkering around on the Carrutherses' automobiles. He wanted to learn to work on them as well as drive them.

"He's very smart," Dvora told Carrie, "and a very hard worker. I believe Mr. Carruthers likes him a great deal."

"He must trust him as well as like him," Carrie said, "if he allows him to work on his expensive cars."

Here in the apartment, Dvora could ask all kinds of questions that she was unable to ask during class time. The lessons helped clear up a great deal of confusion about words, phrases, concepts, and numbers. In just a few weeks, Dvora was making excellent progress.

One afternoon, just as they were finishing up, Carrie happened to ask Dvora about the family she'd left behind in Russia. "Did you have brothers and sisters?" she asked. When she saw the look on Dvora's face, she almost wished she hadn't asked.

"I once had two brothers," she said. "A happy, loving family we were. Money we had little, but love we had plenty." Then she told Carrie how the Russian peasants had been taught to hate and fear the Jews. That brought on severe persecution. Dvora's older brother was forced to leave home and serve in the army.

"It was a sad time to have Isaac leave us," she said. "When Isaac went away, it was the first time I ever saw my papa weep openly. That sadness," she added, "was but the beginning."

In halting words, she told how the peasants came and burned their village. As her family and others fled from the fire, a peasant snatched Dvora's baby brother from her mother's arms.

"Papa told me to run to the forest and not look back," she said, her fists clenched tight, her lips white. "We were told to keep absolutely silent lest we be discovered and all killed. Mama had to swallow all her grief. Her sobs were locked inside her throat."

"Did they keep your baby brother?" Carrie's own eyes were wet with tears.

Dvora shook her head. "Papa told me much later that they'd killed him."

"A little baby?"

"Papa says hate can do that."

Carrie's mind turned to the Klansmen in their very own city who feasted on hate. "What did you do then? How did you live?"

"We slept in the forest for two nights, eating nuts and berries as we could find them. Every moment, we were afraid of being found. I have an awful fear of snakes. One night, as I tried to sleep on the ground, one slithered over my leg, and I screamed. Papa grabbed me and clapped his hand over my mouth."

Dvora stopped a moment to take a drink from her glass of tea. "Which frightened me more, I am not sure—the snake or Papa having to be rough with me."

"Then what happened?"

"Papa said we couldn't stay there any longer. He decided we would walk to another village where my aunt and uncle lived. It was a long way, and Mama was so heartbroken—I thought she would die from grief alone. We walked for many miles. My feet burned like fire, but Papa would not let us rest."

Carrie shook her head. Never could she imagine such a horrible thing. "You found your aunt and uncle?"

Dvora nodded. "They knew people who helped us to get out. Because of the unrest in the country, Mama had sewn our few rubles into the hem of her dress. She was never without our money. Others of our friends lost their money when they fled, but Mama's wisdom saved us. With these rubles, we purchased our way to America. But then. . ."

Dvora could go no further. Carrie moved closer and put her arm about Dvora's shoulder. "It's all right, Dvora. It's all right to cry now. You can weep for all your loved ones now."

And the girl did. Eventually, she said through her sobs, "Many times I have wished that the sickness on the ship might have taken me, as well. It is lonely without Mama and Papa and my brothers."

"But you didn't die. God spared you, Dvora. He brought you to America. God surely has a purpose for your life here."

Dvora nodded, dabbing at her eyes with a handkerchief. Looking at Carrie, she said, "You are right, Carrie. I believe my papa would say the very same thing if he were here."

Carrie noticed the time. "I must go now, Dvora. Thank you for telling me your story. I'm sorry it was so difficult for you." She stood and began putting on her coat.

"Difficult perhaps," Dvora said, "but somehow I feel a little better. Not so heavy." She moved her shoulders to show the heaviness was gone.

"That's what happens when we share a load with another person."

Dvora smiled. "May I hug you, Carrie?" she asked shyly.

"I think friends should hug one another," Carrie said. And she gave her new friend a warm hug. Picking up her books from the table, she hurried outside.

As she walked home in the crisp fall air, these lines went through her head:

Alone in the forest with God as my guide,
*   I moved ever forward with no place to hide.*
But God never failed me,
*   Though dangers assailed me,*
And He safely led me where freedom abides.

In her room that evening, Carrie wrote the words neatly on a piece of tablet paper, signing her name at the bottom. The next day, she found Dvora in the fifth-grade classroom before school started. Mrs. Harwell was at her desk, and only a few other students milled about the room. Garvey was there early because it was his turn to take care of the terrarium.

Carrie stepped up to Dvora and handed her the sheet of paper containing the poem.

Dvora was improving in her ability to read English. She scanned the page and then smiled, her eyes shining bright. "For me?" she said. "It is so very lovely. You wrote this just for me?"

"It's *about* you," Carrie said, "and it's *for* you. Both."

"No one ever wrote a poem especially for me. Never," Dvora said.

"Now someone has."

Just then, Garvey, ever the practical joker, lifted the garter snake from the terrarium. "Hey, girls," he shouted. "Think fast!" As he said the words, he flung the small snake as though he were going to throw it on them.

Dvora's eyes grew wide and terror-filled. She let out a strangled kind of shriek and crumpled to the floor in a heap.

"Garvey, you hateful thing!" Carrie said. "How could you be so cruel?" She knelt beside her friend, and Mrs. Harwell came rushing over.

"I think she's fainted," Mrs. Harwell said. "Garvey, since you were the cause of all this, hurry and fetch us some wet paper towels. Susan," she said to another girl, "bring a glass of water for us."

"I wasn't going to throw the old snake," Garvey said in a pitiful tone. "Honest I wasn't." He put the striped snake back into the terrarium and hurried off to bring the towels.

As she knelt over Dvora, Carrie whispered to her teacher, "She's terrified of snakes." Her teacher nodded in understanding.

In a few moments, Dvora's eyelashes fluttered, and she opened her eyes. She looked ashamed. "I am so sorry," she kept repeating.

Mrs. Harwell shushed her. "You are not the one who should be apologizing," she said. "It's Garvey."

Once Dvora had her wits about her and was sitting in her seat, and once school was taken up and order had been restored, Mrs. Harwell lectured the class about practical jokes and excessive teasing.

"We never know when our teasing, which we think is very funny, is deeply wounding another person," she told them. Then she made Garvey apologize to Dvora in front of the whole class.

Carrie sensed that Garvey was truly sorry. He'd never seen one of his jokes backfire so dramatically. It was a hard lesson.

In the time since Carrie had been friends with Vi and Nate, she'd seen Mrs. Oriel Simmons only a few times. The Bickersons' aunt was a tall, regal-looking woman who stood ramrod straight. Most old people who Carrie knew were bent over, but not Oriel Simmons. She wore her white hair piled high upon her head and wore black dresses with high collars, long sleeves, and skirts that swept the floor. Garvey said she looked as though she'd been caught in the 1800s and never moved forward a day.

One afternoon, Carrie chanced to meet Mrs. Simmons again. She and Vi were playing in the attic, and Carrie had gone up into the turret. Although it was a cold day, the sun was shining brightly. From the window, Carrie could see Dvora playing with her kitten—which wasn't such a little kitten anymore—near the Carrutherses' garden gate.

As she watched, Mrs. Simmons emerged from the back porch of her house with a long, fringed black shawl about her shoulders. She strolled out as though going for a walk. Then a strange thing happened. Mrs. Simmons approached Dvora. The girl never moved. When Mrs. Simmons drew near, the old woman reached out and rested her hand on top of Dvora's head. They stood like that for a brief moment. Then Mrs. Simmons turned and went back into the house.

Carrie pondered what she'd seen, but she told not a soul.

CHAPTER 12

To Detroit

"Carrie, my girl, how would you like to fly in an airplane to Detroit?" Father asked her at supper one evening. "You and your cousin Garvey."

Carrie shivered with delicious excitement. This meant Father had finally convinced his boss that a radio station held enough merit to at least be investigated. But for him to invite her and Garvey—that was a surprise twist. "You want Garvey and me to go along with you?" she asked. "In an airplane?"

"Oh, Glendon," Mother said, "are you sure you know what you're doing? Taking two children along with you?"

"Wait'll I tell Garvey," Carrie said, paying no attention to Mother's remark. "May I call him right now and tell him?"

"It'll be all right, Ida," Father said. "I seem to remember a young girl who was always having misadventures on family trips. If I managed to keep track of her when I was just a boy, I think I can handle my daughter and her cousin."

Carrie looked in amazement as Mother blushed. Could Father be talking about Mother when she was a girl?

Father winked at Carrie and said, "I think you should finish your supper first. Then we'll drive over and tell Garvey. I want to see the look on his face."

Carrie bounced in her chair. "Oh yes! That's a splendid idea!"

Then she stopped for a minute. "But, Father, won't Larry be jealous?"

"Larry's been flying for several weeks now," Father told her. "It's high time Garvey had a turn."

"When is it?" Carrie wanted to know. "When will we fly to Detroit?"

"Next Friday morning." He finished off the last of his coffee and pushed back from the table.

"I'll have to miss a day of school."

"That's right," Father said, "but this will be an education you can't get in the classroom."

The look on Garvey's face was indeed worth waiting for. Carrie couldn't remember him ever being so excited. He was ready to go right then. Later, while the adults were talking in the kitchen, Carrie said to Garvey, "I know I'll be so afraid. I'll probably wither up into a little grease spot right there on the airplane."

"Naw, you won't," Garvey said. "Not with me there to calm you down."

"You won't be afraid?"

Garvey shook his head. "Not one bit. Not a tiny smidgen. Why, Larry's been up a bunch of times, and he says it's great. Nothin' to it. One time, the pilot even let him take the controls. By this time next year, Larry'll be a full-fledged pilot."

"Maybe one day he'll have his very own airplane," Carrie put in.

"Maybe so. Then we can fly with him all the time."

"Well, I'll have to get over my nervousness first," she admitted.

Early Friday morning, as Mother drove the three of them out to the airport, Carrie's stomach was doing crazy flip-flops. Father had suggested she not eat much breakfast. She was glad she had taken his advice.

Garvey was talking a mile a minute all the way out to the airport, barely pausing to take a breath. Not only would they be flying in an airplane, but they would also be staying the night in a hotel room. Carrie had never stayed in a hotel before. Garvey hadn't either.

Larry was already out at the airport when they arrived. He came over to the car to greet them, pointing out the four-seater plane that would take them up. The day was clear and calm, and Larry pronounced it perfect flying weather. Then he happened to look at Carrie.

"You look pale as a ghost," he said with a smile.

"Aw!" Garvey said in a pitiful tone. "We have a fraidy cat going on the trip with us." He put his hands on Carrie's shoulders and turned her about. "Turn around here, Cousin. Let's see how wide that yellow streak really is."

"I'll be all right," Carrie said in a not-too-convincing tone.

"Well, you go right ahead and be scared," Garvey told her. Then jabbing his thumb at his chest, he added, "Me, I'm planning to have a swell time up there."

"You'll both have a swell time," Larry told them.

Carrie could only hope he was right.

Mother walked out to the airplane with them and hugged each of them good-bye.

"I'll telephone you," Father told her, "just as soon as we're settled in at the hotel." He gave her a kiss; then they climbed up into the airplane. Father sat in the front by the pilot, a lanky young man whose name was Edward Maddox. Carrie had heard Larry talk about Ed before. Ed Maddox had been a fighter pilot during the war, shooting down more than a dozen German planes.

Carrie and Garvey sat in the two seats right behind Father and Ed. The small pieces of luggage were stowed in the back. They'd been told earlier to pack light.

The door slammed shut, making Carrie shudder. Because the nose of the plane sat up higher, she was unable to see what Ed was doing at the controls, so she peered out the little window beside her. There was Mother standing by the Chandler Six. Carrie smiled and waved, and Mother waved back. She could see Larry heaving down on the big propeller. Suddenly the noisy motor sprang to life, and the plane inched forward.

"We take her clear to the end of the runway," Ed said over the noise of the motor, "and then turn her around."

Carrie found she was gripping the arm of the seat as tightly as she could. The plane bumped and bounced along the ground, then turned around just as Ed described. He revved up the motors, and they gained momentum. Carrie's breath caught in her throat as they went faster and faster. In a moment, like magic, the plane lifted. Then it lifted a little more, over the tops of the trees, over the roofs of the houses. She gazed in wonderment as they sailed over the top of downtown Minneapolis.

"Oh, Garvey, look!" she exclaimed, pointing to the neat rows of tall office buildings along Washington Avenue. She turned to see if Garvey saw what she was pointing at. But Garvey wasn't looking out the window. His head was lolling back against the seat. His face was pale, and his breath was coming in short gasps. He clutched at his midsection with both hands.

"Father," Carrie said, reaching up to touch her father's arm. "I think Garvey's going to be sick. I mean," she added, "I think he *is* sick!"

Ed turned around and grinned. "Happens to the best of us, chum," he said to Garvey. He handed back a bag that felt all waxy on the outside. "Use this if you need to."

At first, Carrie wasn't sure what he meant. Then it hit her. He meant for Garvey to use it if he needed to throw up. She handed the bag over to Garvey. He took it from her, but he wouldn't look at her.

Carrie didn't feel sick at all. And all her feelings of fear had disappeared. They were flying through tiny bits of clouds that looked just like fluffs of cotton. Down below, the land stretched out like a quilt with colorful patches here and there. Roads crisscrossed the land, and streams and rivers meandered through it. The awesome beauty nearly took her breath away. The most beautiful part was when they flew over Lake Michigan. The sun on the water sparkled like diamonds.

When they were on the ground in Detroit, Garvey was as frisky as ever. But later, as they waited for Carrie's father to check them into the hotel, he begged her not to tell his brother Larry about it.

"He'll never let me live it down," he said. "And don't tell Nate either," he added quickly.

"I promise, Garvey," she said solemnly. "I won't tell a soul."

She wanted to remind him of how he had accused her of having a yellow streak down her back, but she kept quiet. Poor Garvey had suffered enough.

Once their luggage was put away in their room, they took a taxicab from the hotel to the newspaper office. "To the office of the *Detroit News*," Father told the man, as the three of them piled into the backseat.

"Right away, Jake," the man answered.

Garvey chuckled at that.

It wasn't far from the hotel to the tall building that housed the *Detroit News*. When Father paid the cab fare, the man said, "Righto, Jake," and whizzed away.

"He must call everyone Jake," Carrie said laughing. For the rest of the day, she and Garvey kept calling one another Jake. "Righto, Jake," they said to each other, then burst into giggles.

Father took them up the elevator to the eighth-floor office of the man in charge of station 8MK. His name was Ralph Anderssen. Carrie and Garvey had to wait in the reception area while Father and Mr. Anderssen talked. But presently the two men emerged, and it was time to go see the station located on the second floor.

The station wasn't at all what Carrie expected it to be. About the size of the Ruhles' front room, the station walls were hung with thick drapes all the way around. The floor was covered wall to wall with thick carpet.

"This," Ralph explained as he touched one of the curtains, "is to absorb the other sounds in the room so all we hear is the voice at the microphone."

A white grand piano was off to one side, and a large microphone stood out in the center. Along one wall was a long table where the controls were located. It looked somewhat like Sonny's setup in the Simmonses' basement, only larger and cleaner—more neatly arranged. There were dials, meters, knobs, wires, tubes, and headphones.

Garvey's eyes were about to bug out of his head. "A real station," he kept saying in a whisper. "A real radio station."

"You kids come and sit down over here," Ralph Anderssen said, pointing to several chairs sitting against the wall near the controls.

"We're going to air a program shortly."

"Air a program? Honest?" Garvey said.

Ralph laughed. "Honest," he said.

The program was only a lady playing the piano while a man stood close by playing the violin, but it didn't matter. What did matter was that it was a real show, and Carrie and Garvey were right there. "Wait'll Nate hears about this," Garvey whispered to Carrie.

Ralph stood at the microphone and announced the musical numbers, and another man sat at the controls and worked all the knobs and meters and dials. Father watched over his shoulder to see how he operated the system.

When the music was over, Ralph gave a newscast by reading a page of news items into the microphone. At the beginning of the newscast, he said, "Hello, all you folks out there in radio land." At the end, he said, "Tune in tomorrow, same time, same station for the late-breaking news tips on Detroit 8MK."

Then it was all over.

Ralph came to the hotel that evening and treated them all to supper in the hotel restaurant. One would never have suspected that Garvey had been sick. He ate like a horse. While Carrie enjoyed eating out in a nice hotel restaurant, she enjoyed even more hearing Father talk excitedly with Ralph about the radio station. She was sure he wanted to start one at the *Tribune*.

The next morning, they rose early. Ed said a storm might be brewing and he wanted to beat the storm back to Minneapolis.

Privately, Garvey admitted to Carrie that he wasn't too thrilled about getting back into the airplane.

"At least this time you'll know," she said. "So don't eat much breakfast."

He nodded his agreement. However, on the way home, the air was bumpy, and the little plane jostled and jerked. Garvey didn't just turn white. He turned green, as well.

CHAPTER 13

Thanksgiving

Miss Tilden let Carrie begin practicing Christmas music midway through November. Carrie had been asking because she adored Christmas carols and was anxious to learn to play them. She'd already asked Aunt Frances if she might play for the family on Christmas Day. Aunt Frances said that it would be a nice addition to their festivities.

Finally, Miss Tilden gave Carrie the name of a book to purchase at the music store that contained nothing but Christmas music. Carrie was delighted. She'd even attempted to play several numbers at home without Miss Tilden's help. Her ability to read music was steadily improving.

The first day that Carrie used the book during her lessons, she thought about Miss Tilden and the fact that she didn't believe in God. Curiously, she asked, "Miss Tilden, do you decorate your house for the Christmas holidays?" She didn't know if a person who didn't believe in God would do such a thing.

Miss Tilden assured her that of course she decorated for Christmas. "I put up a tree and have tinsel and gaudy lights. Why, sometimes I even put out a bowl of ribbon candy."

Carrie wasn't sure if her teacher was kidding with her or not. But she guessed it didn't matter. Opening the book of Christmas songs, she asked Miss Tilden where she should begin.

"Since this is your choice of music, I'll let you start with the one you like best," her teacher said.

Carrie quickly flipped pages to "Joy to the World."

"This one is my favorite," she said.

"By all means, let's begin with your favorite." Miss Tilden set and wound the metronome.

Carrie played the piece through several times with Miss Tilden making notes on the pages and demonstrating to Carrie ways to improvise with the chords on the left hand.

"Want to know why I like this Christmas carol the best?" Carrie asked.

"I suppose you'd tell me whether I wanted to know or not," quipped Miss Tilden.

"I like it because it tells the message of Christmas in just a few words. It tells us that the Lord Jesus came to earth at Christmas, and we are to make room for Him in our hearts. He came to overturn the curse of the Fall caused by Adam's sin."

"All right, all right, Preacher Caroline. I think that's enough," Miss Tilden said impatiently. "What's your next favorite?"

Flipping through the pages again, Carrie came to "I Heard the Bells on Christmas Day." She liked this one because of the fourth verse, where it said, "Then pealed the bells more loud and deep, 'God is not dead, nor doth He sleep. . . .' " Surely that song would touch Miss Tilden's heart and help her to know that God loved her.

But there seemed to be no reaction from her teacher. Only instructions about chording, rhythm, and volume.

When the lesson was over and Carrie had on her red wool coat and warm knit hat, she turned to Miss Tilden and said, "I think it's awfully nice of you."

"What do you mean, Carrie?"

"It's awfully nice of you to celebrate Jesus' birthday even if you don't know about His Father." Then she turned and went out the door.

As she tripped down the stairs, she hummed to herself, *Melt the clouds of sin and sadness; drive the dark of doubt away. . . .*

"You don't have to eat your Thanksgiving dinner with a baby in your lap," Aunt Frances said with a chuckle.

The Ruhles, the Maurers, the Albrights, and the Constables were all crowded about the large dining room table at the Constable house. Elbows were hitting other elbows, but no one complained. Four-year-old Felix and three-year-old Patricia were at a smaller table close by the kitchen door. The high chair sat empty over in the corner.

Carrie scooped up another bite of yummy mashed potatoes and giblet gravy, then gave Joey a squeeze. "But I want to hold him," she said. "And besides, he likes sitting on my lap, don't you, Joey?" As though to answer, the toddler wiggled and gave a squeal.

"Caroline," Mother said, "please don't talk with your mouth full."

"Sorry," Carrie said.

Liese laughed. "Every time that baby is around Carrie, he gets more and more spoiled."

"That's not true," Carrie protested. "Aunt Frances helps a lot."

"So do I," Gloria chimed in.

"And me," Edie echoed.

By now everyone was laughing.

"All right, all right," Liese said. "I have to face the fact that everyone in the family is helping to spoil our son."

Father, still excited about his Detroit trip, described the station in detail. And again there was a discussion about the pros and cons of commercials on the radio.

In the midst of the conversation, Edie turned to Garvey and asked, "Well, tell us, Garvey, how was the airplane ride? We haven't heard from you yet."

Carrie watched as Garvey ducked his head and pretended to be very interested in buttering a fat yeast roll. "It was okay, I guess."

"Okay?" said Don, Liese's husband. "You rode all the way from Minneapolis to Detroit on your first plane ride, and it was only okay?"

Carrie watched closely to see how her cousin would handle this.

Slowly, Garvey looked up at all the family members and said, "I got real sick. So sick I threw up." His face was pink with embarrassment, but at least he'd been honest. Carrie was proud of him.

At that moment, Larry spoke up. "Garvey," he said, "did I ever tell you—the same thing happened to me my first time up."

Garvey's face registered astonishment. "No kidding? You got sick?"

"Cross my heart." Larry crisscrossed his finger over his shirt pocket. "A lot of people do, you know."

"No, I didn't know." Garvey glanced at Carrie and smiled.

"Well, it's true. So don't feel bad about it."

Garvey looked as though someone had opened a cage door and set him free.

Edie turned to Carrie. "How's your tutoring coming along?" she asked.

By now, everyone in the extended family knew about Carrie's project with Dvora. "Just great. Dvora's grades are steadily climbing.

Since we're in the same class, I see things that give her problems, and then we work on those areas." Carrie paused to give Joey a little bite of turkey dressing, and he chewed it happily.

"Mrs. Harwell keeps close tabs on what we're doing," Carrie continued, "and she gives me ideas on how to present the concepts."

"What a blessing that you're right there to be her friend," Edie told her. "It's no fun being different from all the other kids."

Liese nodded her agreement. "We Maurer children were called all sorts of not-so-nice names during the Great War," she said. "Not only were we called names, but sometimes the kids just ignored us. And for no more reason than our German name. That's how ridiculous prejudice can be."

Carrie caught Garvey's attention to make sure he'd heard those words, but he quickly looked away. She'd be sure to remind him of his cousins' statements the next time he sided with Nate about Dvora.

By this time, Carrie's knowledge of Jewish holidays was growing. From Dvora, she'd learned about the High Holy Days in the early fall when Yom Kippur (the Day of Atonement) and Rosh Hashanah (the Jewish New Year) were followed closely by the Feast of Tabernacles or the Ingathering. She asked Dvora questions about them, then went home and, with Father's help, looked them up in the Old Testament.

"It's amazing," Father said. "Amazing that these feast days have been kept alive for thousands of years."

"Mr. Clausen told me that each of these feasts were fulfilled in Jesus," Carrie said. "For example, Yom Kippur is the Day of Atonement. When Jesus died on the cross, He atoned for our sins.

I like the way it all fits together."

Her father was quiet for a time. When she looked over at him, he was gazing off into space. "It certainly does all fit together, doesn't it?"

Even more interesting than the feasts was the way Dvora and her uncle observed the Sabbath, or Shabbat, every week.

"Gentiles believe a day begins in the morning," Dvora once told Carrie, "but in the Torah, it says, 'And the evening and the morning were the first day.' It names evening first. So our day begins at evening, and our Shabbat observance begins at sundown on Friday and ends at sundown on Saturday."

Dvora went on to explain how they lit the Shabbat candles and prayed. On the Sabbath, they did no work nor were they supposed to travel any distance.

Carrie went home and looked in the book of Genesis. Sure enough, it did say evening first. But somehow she still liked to think of her day ending when she fell asleep and beginning when she first awoke. She was also thankful that she could go to Saturday matinees at the movies and did not have to stay inside all day and observe the Sabbath as Dvora did.

"We'll cut out our construction-paper Santas, our angels, and our snowmen," Mrs. Harwell instructed the class. "Then we'll unroll the cotton matting from this package." She held the box up that had a red cross on the side. "You can tear strips of cotton and glue them to your picture however you please. When you're finished, we'll post them on the bulletin boards around the room."

Snow was falling outside the large classroom windows, which made Carrie even more excited about the approach of Christmas.

In spite of bad weather, the students kept the bird-feeding station clear of the snow and kept seed out for the winter birds. Just then, a cardinal had come up to the feeder, its bright red feathers contrasting against the white snow.

Carrie carefully cut out her fat, jovial Santa. She cut out black boots and a black belt and pasted them on, using the thick paste from the jar in her desk. When she was ready for the cotton, she went to Mrs. Harwell's desk to tear off the needed strips. Only then did she glance over at Dvora. The girl's face was sad. Almost as sad as it had been when she first arrived. She was not cutting or pasting. She was just sitting there.

Carrie was glad it was their lesson night at the garage apartment. There, in the quiet of Dvora's home, Carrie could ask her Jewish friend what was wrong.

"I cannot celebrate your Christmas," Dvora said softly. "I have read the words of the songs of your Christmas. The Christ Child is not my Lord. The God of heaven, the God of Israel is my Lord."

"Oh, I see," Carrie said. Why hadn't she thought of that?

"We will be celebrating Hanukkah. We also call it the Festival of Lights."

"Tell me about it," Carrie said. "Tell me about the Festival of Lights. It has such a nice sound."

"A nice sound, yes. But before the 'nice,' there was death and destruction. Years before Jesus was born, the Jews were taken over by a wicked man named Antiochus from Syria. He demanded that all the people of Judah become Greek and bow to Zeus, their Greek god. Mean soldiers from Syria destroyed the sacred Temple in Jerusalem and demanded that the Jews eat of the pigs they had killed there, which was against our Law. One brave man refused to do so. His name was Mattathias."

"Almost like the story of Shadrach, Meshach, and Abednego," Carrie said, "when they wouldn't bow to Nebuchadnezzar."

"Yes, like that," Dvora agreed. Just then, a little mew sounded from the corner as Vanya rose from her bed in the corner and came to rub on Dvora's leg. Dvora reached down, picked up the kitten, and snuggled her in her lap.

"This man Mattathias," Dvora went on, "had five sons. His sons joined him in a long fight against the Syrians. Soon other brave men joined them, until they had a small army up in the hills outside the city. There was much killing, but the Maccabees, as they called themselves, held out."

"Weren't they greatly outnumbered?" Carrie asked.

Dvora nodded. "They were. But the Lord was on their side and brought the miracle they needed. After years of fighting, the Maccabees at last returned to Jerusalem in triumph. But the Temple, oh, the lovely Temple." Tears filled Dvora's eyes. "Dirt, blood, ashes everywhere."

"How terrible," Carrie said, caught up in the story. "Did they clean it up?"

"They did. But there was no oil for the menorah. The candle-stand with the seven branches was to burn in the Temple continually, but the Syrians had put out the flames. It was important that the menorah burn brightly once again. It required a special clean and holy oil. There was none."

Dvora stroked her kitten, its noisy purring filling the air.

"Then what happened?" Carrie asked.

"Enough oil was found to burn the menorah for one day. They prayed and asked the Lord for more time. Time to prepare more oil. The Lord answered their prayers. The menorah burned another day. And another."

"With just the first little bit of oil?" Carrie asked.

Dvora nodded.

"How did it do that?"

Dvora smiled. "The Lord's miracle. It burned for eight full days. During those days, enough oil was prepared to keep it burning." Pointing to a nine-branched candlestick up on a high shelf, she said, "Up there is Uncle's menorah. We light one candle each day."

"What's the ninth candle for?" Carrie asked.

"We call it the 'helper' candle, or *shammes*. It is used to light the other eight."

"So that's why the menorah is so important. It helps you remember the miracle of the oil," Carrie said.

"The menorah reminds us of the miracle of the oil," Dvora agreed, "and all of Hanukkah reminds us of the faithfulness of the Lord. Now you see why we celebrate for eight days."

Carrie smiled. "That's longer than our one day of Christmas."

Dvora went to a chest that sat against one wall. It was painted blue with brightly colored flowers decorating the front. Opening a drawer, she pulled out a small object and brought it back to the table where they studied.

"Why, it's a top," Carrie said when Dvora had set it on the table.

"We call it a *dreidel*," her friend corrected. "When the wicked Antiochus ordered the Jews to no longer study the Torah, they did so in secret. When they heard soldiers coming, they hid their scrolls and brought out the dreidels and pretended to have a game."

Dvora gave the dreidel a spin. "This one belongs to Uncle Yerik," she said. "Our family dreidel was lost when our cottage burned. We play games with the top, spinning to see which letter is on top when it stops spinning."

"We should tell Mrs. Harwell about all of this, Dvora."

But Dvora wasn't finished. "Also during Hanukkah, we eat *latkes*, or potato pancakes. Cooked in oil, they remind us of the oil the Lord provided for the lamp. Mmm," she said, thinking about it. "After we were driven from our home, when I was very hungry, I dreamed of eating latkes. When I came here, Uncle Yerik fixed them for me just special, even though Hanukkah was many months away."

"Are you happy here, Dvora?" Carrie asked.

Dvora took a moment to answer. "I wanted so much for Mama and Papa to be here with me. But Uncle Yerik gives to me of his love. We are blessed with the kindness of Mr. and Mrs. Carruthers."

She looked at Carrie and smiled. "Your many kindnesses, too," she added. Then she said, "And the kind old lady who lives in the big house where you play with Violet. She, too, has spread happiness to me."

The comment about Mrs. Simmons puzzled her, but Carrie asked no more questions.

As they set about to study, Carrie kept thinking about Hanukkah. By the time she was ready to leave, she said to Dvora, "First thing tomorrow, I'll talk to Mrs. Harwell about your Hanukkah. I'm sure she'll understand."

Mrs. Harwell agreed that Dvora shouldn't have to sing songs about Christmas if she didn't want to. Then she suggested that Dvora give a talk to the class about Hanukkah, its meaning, and how it is celebrated.

Dvora shook her head. "I am too frightened to stand in front of all the eyes in the class."

"What if I stood beside you?" Carrie suggested.

Dvora thought a moment. "If my friend were with me, then I would be brave enough to do it."

CHAPTER 14

The Accident

Vi never let it be a secret that she did not like Dvora Levinsky. It made for many unpleasant and awkward moments at school. Dvora even said to Carrie one day, "I am sorry your friend Violet does not like me. Perhaps you should be friends with only her."

Carrie wasn't sure what to say. Sometimes she felt she wasn't being a very good friend to either one of them. Dvora still spent many lonely hours by herself at recess. No one invited her to play with them. Although Carrie longed to include her, she was certain Vi would never stand for it.

At the same time, Vi was having other problems and with Nate, of all people. Opal had asked Vi why Nate was going off with Sonny late at night.

"What could I say?" Vi asked Carrie with a worried look in her eyes. "It was the first I'd known anything about it."

"But I thought Nate didn't even like Sonny."

Vi gave a shrug. They were walking around the snow-covered playground together during recess. "I think he wants very much to impress Sonny. To do that, he has to tag along."

"Where do you think they go?"

"Oh, Carrie," Vi said, her voice trembling. "I think they go to Klan meetings."

Carrie thought about that. "Maybe it's time to talk to your aunt

Oriel." Carrie was sure that's what she would do if she were Violet.

But Vi disagreed. "I could never bother Aunt Oriel. Opal says she doesn't want to be bothered. Ever."

Carrie thought that was terribly sad.

Dvora did well in her talk to the class about Hanukkah. Carrie knew the girl was terrified. Dvora's voice was soft but steady as she explained about the different aspects of the holiday and what it meant to her and her family. The night before, at Dvora's kitchen table, Carrie had helped her draw pictures of the menorah and the dreidel. Now as Dvora spoke, Carrie held up the pictures and gave her friend moral support, of course.

No one was rude to the immigrant girl, because Mrs. Harwell was right there keeping a close watch. But neither did anyone act interested. Later during recess, Vi said she thought Carrie was silly for standing up there with "that Jewish girl," as she called her. Vi hardly ever said Dvora's name.

The Christmas tree at the Ruhles' house was so loaded with gifts that Carrie was almost embarrassed. Garvey told her if there were four kids in her family instead of just one, she'd never get so many toys.

On Christmas morning, she opened gift after gift. She received a new doll and doll buggy, a doll cradle complete with a pretty lacy pillow and coverlet, a six-room dollhouse with all the miniature furniture, and a set of watercolors. There were games and new clothes, too. How Carrie wished she could share a few of her new things with Dvora, who had so little.

Not that she wasn't grateful. In fact, she thanked her parents several times for all the nice things. But she was glad when it was time to go to Aunt Frances's house for dinner. She was happiest when the families were all together. That, to her, was more important than all the presents in the world. How awful it would be to have no parents at all. Like Dvora. Like Violet and Nate.

When dinner was over and the dishes were cleaned up, Aunt Frances announced to the family that Carrie would be playing the piano for them. The radio was switched off, and Carrie sat down and began to play the Christmas carols that she loved so. She hadn't gone far when voices began to join in. Before she knew it, the family was standing around the piano, singing with great gusto. They asked her to play another and another.

"We used to do this years ago," Uncle Kenneth said later. "I wonder why we ever stopped?"

"Perhaps it's because of a thing called *radio*," Aunt Frances quipped.

Throughout the day, Carrie kept an eye out for an opportunity to talk to Aunt Frances privately. She wanted to ask her aunt's opinion about this problem with Vi. Her chance came late in the afternoon. There was a new drama featured on the radio, which had captured everyone's attention. Aunt Frances had been rocking Patty, and the little girl was nearly asleep. Baby Joseph was already sleeping on the bed in the downstairs bedroom.

Liese said, "Aunt Frances, she's too heavy for you to hold. I'll take her upstairs and put her in Felix's bed."

"No, no," Aunt Frances said. "I'll do it. You sit down and enjoy a rest."

Carrie jumped up from the floor where she'd been playing with her new doll. "I'll come with you, Aunt Frances."

"That would be nice," she said. "Come along then."

Felix still slept in a bed with sides on it. Carrie went into the room first and let down the side and pulled down the covers so Aunt Frances could lay Patty down. "Thank you, Carrie. You're such a good helper."

When Patty was tucked in and the two came back out into the hallway, Carrie said, "Before we go downstairs, Aunt Frances, may I ask you something?"

Her aunt smiled. "So there was more to this trip than just helping your old aunt?"

"Oh, no," Carrie said. "I would have helped you anyway."

"I'm teasing you. Of course you would. What's your question?"

As briefly as she could, Carrie explained about how Vi had acted ever since Dvora had come to live in the neighborhood. "I want to be friends with both of them, but I don't know how to do it."

"It sounds to me like Violet Bickerson is frightened, Carrie."

"Frightened?"

Aunt Frances nodded. "Does Violet have many friends besides you?"

Carrie shook her head. "We've been best friends since the beginning of fourth grade."

"I don't think Vi really dislikes Dvora. I think she's afraid of losing you as her dear friend."

"Why, that would never happen," Carrie said.

"But Vi doesn't know that," her aunt pointed out.

Carrie nodded. "I see what you mean. What do you think I should do?"

"Perhaps you could think of ways to reassure Violet of your friendship," Aunt Frances suggested. "Maybe your mother would let you invite her over to stay the night. To have a little party, just the two of you."

"Mother doesn't really like to have lots of kids around, you know," Carrie said. "I think too much noise bothers her."

"But you could promise to be quiet."

"Vi and I sometimes get the giggles."

"One fit of giggles isn't going to hurt Ida. I guarantee it," Aunt Frances said, smiling. "She's had fits of giggles in her day."

"Do you really think that might work?"

"It's worth a try. When Violet becomes more sure of your friendship, perhaps Dvora will be less of a threat."

"Oh, Aunt Frances. That's a great idea. Thanks a lot."

The holiday vacation was a perfect time to try her aunt's suggestion. Carrie waited until the day after Christmas, when all the fuss and bother was over. To her surprise, Mother said she thought it was a nice idea to have a friend over. The next step was to call Violet and invite her.

Vi's response was one of surprise. "You want me to come and stay the night? Truly?"

"Truly. Mother says we can listen to a radio program and pop popcorn. It'll be ever so much fun."

"And no school the next day."

"Right. That means we'll have even more fun. I'll let you play with my new dollhouse."

"You have a new dollhouse?" Excitement was growing in Violet's voice.

"Yes, and I want to share it with you."

When they hung up, Carrie wondered why she'd never thought of this before.

Carrie couldn't remember ever having so much fun with Violet.

They played house with the dolls, and then they played house with the big dollhouse. They played board games and listened to radio programs. Mother allowed them to stay up late that night and sleep late the next morning.

Aunt Frances was right—Mother didn't seem to be bothered at all by their noise. It made Carrie wonder why she'd ever thought such a thing in the first place. Best of all, Carrie was able to assure Vi how important their friendship was.

Late in the afternoon of the following day, it came time to pick up all the toys and put them away. They had promised Opal that Vi would be home by supper time.

"I'll walk you home," Carrie told her.

"I was hoping you would," Vi replied.

They bundled up against the cold and walked slowly together in the pale blue of winter dusk.

Vi thanked Carrie several times for the wonderful time they'd had together.

"We'll do it again soon," Carrie promised.

As they approached the Simmonses' house, sounds of Garvey's and Nate's laughing and shouting came floating toward them through the cold winter air.

"Sounds like they're having fun," Vi said.

"I wonder what's up?" Carrie felt a funny kind of anxiousness. She hurried out ahead of Vi, and as she came to the other side of the Carrutherses' house, she saw why. Garvey was teasing Dvora's cat. Dvora, who was up on the apartment steps, made a feeble cry of protest.

Carrie had just opened her mouth to order them to stop, when the cat bolted and made a beeline for the street. At the same moment, a car came careening down the street. As if in a fog, Carrie heard the cat cry and heard Dvora scream.

"Oh no!" Carrie raced out to the street. The car didn't stop. The driver probably didn't even know he'd hit such a small animal. The lovely black-and-white cat lay motionless against the curb. Carrie knelt down and touched its neck. She felt a pulse. There was still life.

"Vanya," Dvora called out amid choking sobs. "My darling Vanya."

"Nathaniel," Carrie called out, "is Sonny home?"

"He's here."

"We need a ride to the veterinarian's. Tell him it's an emergency!"

Dvora pulled off her babushka and wrapped it around the cat. With Carrie's help, they lifted Vanya into Dvora's arms. Dvora looked up at Carrie with tear-filled eyes. "Everyone whom I love dies. Is there no mercy?"

"Vanya's not going to die," Carrie promised. But she had no idea if the cat would live or not.

In a moment, Nate was back out at the curb. Nate was shaking his head, his face ashen. "Says he won't come. Says he wouldn't lift a finger to help any Jew. Even if it's a Jew's cat."

Just as Carrie started to protest, the front door opened. Oriel Simmons came down the front stairs of the house. She was dressed in a long wool coat with a thick fur collar. In her hand was a matching fur muff.

"Nathaniel," she said in a loud stern voice.

"Yes, ma'am?"

"You go tell Sonny to get up here and get that car of his started instantly. Tell him I said so."

"Yes, ma'am."

Mrs. Simmons came over to Dvora. "Come, child. Bring your

pet. Let's get into the car." Looking at Carrie and Violet, she added, "You girls come along. Dvora will need you there."

A disgruntled Sonny came out of the basement wearing only a lightweight jacket and tweed cap. He jumped in his car and drove them to the veterinarian's office. The old jalopy had a rag top on it now, but it was still very cold inside—nothing like the Ruhles' warm car.

Vi rode in the front seat with Sonny, while Mrs. Simmons, Dvora, and Carrie were in the back. As they drove along, Carrie heard Mrs. Simmons whisper something to Dvora. It sounded like *"Doosh-sheesh-ka."*

Carrie acted as though she didn't notice.

Sonny stayed outside while the girls and Mrs. Simmons took the cat into the office. Dvora was trembling with fright. When the kind old veterinarian came out to take Vanya, Dvora didn't want to let go of her beloved pet. "Please, please, don't hurt my Vanya," she said with a sad whimper. "I love her so."

Carrie put her arm around Dvora's shoulder. "This man is a doctor for animals, Dvora. He's going to help make Vanya well."

Dvora still had fear in her eyes.

"You'll have to trust him," Carrie said softly. "Otherwise, Vanya may not make it."

Carrie knew it was a difficult thing for Dvora to do to release Vanya into the hands of this stranger.

"I'll take good care of her," the elderly doctor said gently.

The girls went over to a leather couch and sat down. Vi sat on one side of Dvora and Carrie on the other. Dvora ran her fingers absently over the fringe of the babushka. Mrs. Simmons sat apart from them, her chin up, her back straight, saying nothing.

Carrie wondered if Mrs. Simmons had been watching the entire episode from her window. Why else would she have appeared at just the right moment? And dressed in her coat!

The wait seemed like an eternity. Finally, the vet appeared at the door to the reception area. He came right over to Dvora and reached down to take her hand. "Your pet has had a hard blow, but I believe she's going to be all right. Watch her very carefully tonight. If there are any problems, please call me."

Dvora shook her head.

"They have no telephone," Carrie told him.

"She may use ours," Violet said to the doctor. "I'm her neighbor."

"Very well then," the vet said. "Come this way."

As they followed him down the hall, Dvora whispered to Carrie. "This will cost so much money. Uncle can never pay for such a fine doctor as this."

"We'll worry about that later," Carrie said. She'd already been thinking that she would ask her father to pay the bill. Or perhaps Uncle Ken would make Garvey pay for part of the bill since it was his foolishness that had caused the accident.

Vanya was lying on the table, looking very listless.

"I've given her a sedative to keep her calm," the doctor explained. "It will take some time for it to wear off."

"May I wrap her back up in my babushka?" Dvora asked.

"You certainly may," the vet answered.

When they came back out to the reception area, Mrs. Simmons was standing at the counter paying for the bill from her small, black leather coin purse.

CHAPTER 15

The Popsicle Jingle

When they returned, Sonny was as sullen as ever. He drove up into the Simmonses' driveway, stopped the car, got out, and went back down to the basement.

"Thank you for paying—," Dvora started to say in her quiet voice, but Mrs. Simmons gave a wave of her gloved hand.

"Please forgive the impudence of my grandson and my nephew, my dear. I trust such an unfortunate incident will never happen again." She turned and went inside.

Carrie looked at Vi. "Have you ever. . . ?"

"Never," Vi replied to the unfinished question.

"Such a kind lady, your aunt is," Dvora said. "I'll take Vanya inside now where it is warm."

"Yes," Carrie said. "Want us to walk you to the stairs?"

Dvora shook her head. "Vanya and I, we are fine now."

As she turned to go, the front door of the Simmonses' house opened, and a sheepish Garvey came out.

"There you are," Carrie said. "We'd better get home. It's getting late."

"We will," he said. "But first I need to apologize to Dvora. I never meant for your kitten to be hurt," he said to the Jewish girl. "Mrs. Harwell told me that teasing could hurt someone, and now I see what she means. I'm terribly sorry, Dvora. Will you forgive me?"

Dvora gave a shy little smile. "Never has one asked for forgiveness who has been cruel to me. Thank you for asking. I say yes. I forgive."

Garvey reached out to gently touch the babushka that covered Vanya. "I'm glad she's gonna be all right."

Dvora nodded. "She is all right. I am all right."

Later as Carrie and Garvey were walking home, she began scolding him for what he had done. But then she stopped herself. "You know, Garvey, even though the accident was a terrible thing, God brought good out of it."

He was quiet for a moment and then said, "That's exactly what last week's Sunday school memory verse was about. 'All things work together for good to them that love God. . . .'"

"It's true." Carrie pulled her coat collar up around her neck and walked a little faster against the cold wind. "Vi sat next to Dvora at the vet's office, just as though she were Dvora's friend, too."

They walked along in silence for a time, then Garvey said, "Carrie, I've not been very nice to you when it comes to Dvora. I guess I've just been saying the same thing Nate says because it was safer that way. I didn't want to lose his friendship."

Carrie glanced over at him. His face was serious. "Do you feel differently now?"

Garvey nodded. "I never dreamed that Sonny would be so heartless when the poor kitten was hurt. When I say things, I'm usually just kidding. I don't mean it. When Sonny says it, he really means it."

"But, Garvey. . ."

"Yeah?"

"Whether you mean the words or don't mean the words, they still hurt the one who hears them."

"You sure are right about that, Carrie."

"Righto, Jake," Carrie said. And they both laughed.

It wasn't until Carrie was back home, taking off her hat and coat, that another thought occurred to her. Nate had not shown his face at all after they returned from the vet's office. Why had he not apologized?

In Carrie's opinion, January was of little use except to hold a space between New Year's and Valentine's Day. All the excitement of the holidays was over, and the days were mostly gray and dreary.

At school, Garvey was upset because Nate no longer talked to him.

"Know what he called me?" Garvey asked Carrie one morning before school.

"What?"

"Chicken."

"Why would he do that?"

"Because I apologized to Dvora."

"Any time that I ever had to apologize," Carrie said, "I found it took courage, not cowardice."

Garvey shook his head. "I sure wish it were summer so we could be playing baseball again."

Carrie knew what he meant, but she didn't think a game of baseball was going to help this situation.

Vi, too, was worried about Nate. "He just acts strange," she said.

"What do you mean by strange?" Carrie asked her. They were sitting together at Vi's desk, eating their lunch.

Vi shrugged. "I can't explain it. He's just different. He doesn't talk to me or tell me things like he used to." She squeezed her eyes to shut off the threat of tears. "It never used to matter much that Sonny or Aunt Oriel never spent time with me because I always had Nate. Now this has happened. It makes me feel sort of scared. And lonely," she added.

Carrie hesitated a moment, then she said, "Vi, that's exactly how Dvora feels every day."

Vi looked over at Dvora, who was eating her lunch alone. "I never thought about that," she said. She looked back at Carrie. "Let's take our lunches over there and eat with her."

Carrie smiled. "Let's do!"

One good thing about winter was that Mother and Father were home more. Evenings were spent together in the living room listening to programs on the radio and just being together. On one of those evenings in late January, the telephone rang.

"I hope that's not the *Tribune*," Mother said. She was at her desk typing out letters for one of the clubs she belonged to.

"I hope so, too." Father put down the magazine he'd been reading and got up out of his easy chair. He turned down the volume on the radio console before going to the hall to answer the phone.

From where she was sitting near Mother's desk, Carrie heard her father say, "Popsicle what? Are you sure the name is Caroline Ruhle?"

Mother stopped her typing and looked at Carrie. "What's this all about?"

Carrie shrugged. "I'm not sure."

Then from the hall came Father's voice. "Caroline, do you know anything about a jingle for a radio advertisement for Popsicles?"

Carrie clapped her hand over her mouth. "Oh, my," she said.

Father came to the door of the living room. "Caroline, this man on the phone wants to know if you will sell your jingle for two hundred dollars."

"Carrie," Mother said, "what have you done?"

Carrie started laughing. Garvey must have sent the jingle in— or Violet. "May we call the man back?" she said. "I'll tell you the whole story."

CHAPTER 16
Nolan and Suzette

Both Carrie's parents thought the story of her writing the jingle during the summer was very humorous. She telephoned Garvey to ask him about it, and he confessed to mailing her poem in.

"You ran off that day, remember?" he said. "So Vi and Nate and I wrote it out just as you said it. I didn't think you would ever mail it in, so I did it myself. You aren't mad, are you, Carrie?" he added. "I put your name on it. I'd almost forgotten all about it. And by the way, why are you asking?"

When she told him about the telephone call, he let out a whoop that almost made her drop the telephone. Father laughed. He could hear it several feet away.

"If I sell the jingle," Carrie told her cousin, "I'm going to give you half of the money."

"Wow, Carrie. You don't have to do that."

"I know I don't have to. But if you hadn't sent it in, I would never have sold it."

"Wait until it airs on the radio," Garvey said. "That'll be exciting. We'll tell all the kids at Washington Elementary. You'll be famous."

"I doubt that I'll be famous, Garvey. But it will be fun to hear it on the air."

After hanging up the phone, Carrie said to her father, "I think

I rather agree with you."

"About what?" he asked.

"I think we *should* have commercials on the radio!"

The next day, Father called the man at the Popsicle company and told him that Caroline wanted to sell the jingle, but that the price was $250. Mother said that was because "your father always feels he has to negotiate everything."

Carrie had already decided that not only was she going to share the money with Garvey, but that when it arrived, she would ask her parents if she could give part of it to Dvora, as well. She hoped they would say yes.

In the weeks following Christmas, Miss Tilden had been asking Carrie a few questions about God and about Jesus, but they were strange, adult-sounding questions. How do you really know if the Bible is true? If God is good, where did sin come from in the first place? These were questions Carrie had never thought of before.

"I don't know if I can tell you the answer," Carrie said at one point, "but I'm sure Mr. Clausen would know. Why don't you talk to him?"

Miss Tilden smiled. "I have been talking to him."

Carrie nearly fell off the piano bench. "You have?"

Miss Tilden nodded.

"Then why are you asking me?"

"Because I feel so childish asking him all these things."

Carrie fought hard not to let the excitement she was feeling bubble up and show on the outside. "Miss Tilden, God Himself can answer your questions. The Bible says the Holy Spirit is the best teacher. Do you have a Bible?"

Miss Tilden blushed. "I just bought one."

"That's good," Carrie said. "That's the best place to begin. Before you read, pray and ask God to show you the truths that are there. After all, He should know. He's the Author."

"Thanks, Carrie."

It was Friday, February 15, 1924, the day after Valentine's Day. The Ruhles were just about ready to sit down to supper when there came a knock on the door.

Mother went to answer it. Carrie heard her say, "Why, Mr. Clausen, Miss Tilden. Welcome. Won't you please come in?"

Carrie went running into the front hall. She could hardly believe her eyes. There stood her teachers, and both of them were smiling. And they were holding hands!

Mother was bustling about, taking their coats and hanging them in the front closet. Meanwhile, Father had come into the foyer. Mother made the introductions and then ushered them all into the living room.

"We were just about ready to eat," Mother said. "Won't you join us? We can easily set two more places."

"Thank you, no." Mr. Clausen looked at Miss Tilden. His electric eyes were lit up. "I'm taking Suzette out to dinner. We're going to celebrate."

"And what is the occasion for celebration?" Mother asked.

"I asked Suzette to marry me yesterday. On Valentine's Day," Mr. Clausen told them. "And she accepted."

Now Miss Tilden shyly held out her left hand. There was a small ruby ring on her fourth finger. Carrie could no longer contain her excitement. She ran to Miss Tilden, threw her arms around her neck, and gave her a giant hug. Her piano teacher hugged her right back.

"Your daughter is a dear girl," Miss Tilden said to Carrie's parents. "But my engagement to Nolan, happy as it is, isn't the best news. The best news is that because of Carrie here, I've asked Jesus into my heart."

"Oh, Miss Tilden," Carrie said. "That *is* the best news."

"You were right, Carrie. The Holy Spirit is the best teacher." Looking over at Mr. Clausen, she added, "But Nolan here doesn't do too badly."

"When will this special occasion take place?" Father asked.

"In the summer, after I graduate," Mr. Clausen said. "I've accepted a pastorate at a small church on the outskirts of St. Paul."

Father sat forward in his easy chair and pressed his fingers to his mouth as though he were thinking.

"What is it, dear?" Mother asked him.

"I just had an idea," Father said. "Mr. Clausen, the *Tribune* is starting up a new radio station in the city. My editor is allowing me to set it up and get it rolling. I would very much like our station to include the preaching of God's Word."

"That sounds like a wise decision," Mr. Clausen said. "But why are you telling me?"

"Because I want you to be the one who does it."

"Me?" Mr. Clausen laughed.

Miss Tilden squeezed his hand. "Why, Nolan, that would be perfect. You're always saying how you want to tell everyone about the Lord. Now you can!"

"But on the radio? I don't know anything about—"

Father interrupted him. "None of us knows a thing about what we're doing," he said with a smile. "We're all learning together. I'd like to begin with a short sermon," Father continued. "Say about fifteen minutes, once a week. We'll see how that works, then we can grow from there. What do you say?"

"I'd be a fool to turn down that kind of offer, Mr. Ruhle. And I so appreciate the opportunity. Using the radio to spread the gospel is a smart idea."

"My husband is a smart man," Mother added.

"We really must be going," Mr. Clausen said as he stood up. "But we felt we had to come by and say thank you. If it weren't for Carrie, none of this would have happened. Thank you, Carrie."

Carrie felt her face growing warm. "I just wanted Miss Tilden to know that God loves her," she said. "And for God to drive the dark of doubt away."

Miss Tilden stood beside her fiancé. She reached down to cradle Carrie's face in her hands and kissed her forehead. "God did do just that, Carrie. And it's wonderful. Just like you said!"

Father gave Mr. Clausen the telephone number at his office. "Call me, and we'll set up a time for you to come in and air the show!"

After their guests left, the family moved to the dining room. Mother was unusually quiet as they ate their supper. At length she said, "Glendon, it seems to me our daughter has showed us up."

"I agree with you, Ida."

"We've been guilty of neglecting the Lord in our own home."

"And in our lives," Father added.

"I think we should set about to change things. Do you agree?" Mother asked.

"I certainly do," Father said.

Just then, Carrie jumped up and ran to the living room. Grabbing the family Bible from the table, she brought it back and put it by Father's place.

"Let's begin tonight. Right after supper," she said.

Garvey, Carrie, and Violet had just returned to the Simmonses' house from a Saturday matinee and were playing up in the attic. They'd seen *Rosita*, starring Mary Pickford, so they were all set to play Spanish dancers.

"I wish Nate were here to play with us," Garvey said as he draped a large black cape over his shoulders. "It's never as much fun without him."

"He and Sonny have been coming in later and later at night," Vi said. "Opal's terribly worried about him."

"He's been spending more time with Sonny?" Garvey asked.

Vi nodded. "It's as though he finally found a way to get Sonny's attention."

"Shh," Carrie said. "It sounds like the door downstairs."

Sure enough, the door at the second-floor entrance opened and closed again.

"Nate?" Vi called out. "Is that you?"

"Yeah, it's me." His voice sounded strange.

When his head appeared at the stairwell, Carrie, Vi, and Garvey stared at him in disbelief. Nate's eyes were red as though he'd been crying. Carrie couldn't imagine Nathaniel Bickerson crying. What would ever make him cry?

"Nate, old pal," Garvey said, acting as though nothing were amiss. "You're here at last. Just in time, too. We have a great game started. We just got back from seeing *Rosita*, and now we're ready to play—"

"I can't play with you, Garvey," Nate said, his tone gruff. "There's something I gotta do."

"Then why. . . ?" Garvey started. But Vi waved him quiet.

She walked over to her brother. "Nate, what's wrong? You look like you've been crying. Are you all right?"

"I don't guess I'll ever be all right again," he said. He pressed at his eyes with his fingers, but the tears came anyway.

"Does it have to do with Sonny?" Vi asked.

Nate nodded.

"And the Klan?" Carrie put in.

He nodded again. "I felt real special when Sonny first asked me to go to a meeting with him. He'd never paid the least bit of attention to me before. I wanted him to like me. I wanted him to be proud of me."

"Oh, Nate," Vi said, her voice full of compassion.

"But after I went one time, then he wanted me to go again. And again. Then he paid my dues for me to join the Klan."

"You went and joined the Ku Klux Klan?" Garvey asked in disbelief.

Carrie could hardly believe it herself.

"I had no choice," Nate told them. "Sonny said I'd seen too much and heard too much not to join up."

"That can't be true," Carrie said. But she didn't really know if it were true or not.

"Anyway, now I'm in. The meetings are real scary. They talk about doing all kinds of awful things to people. Tonight I gotta do an awful thing. Like an initiation."

They were all quiet. Then Vi asked, "What awful thing, Nate?"

"I have to take a live chicken, cut its throat, and lay it on the Levinskys' doorstep."

Carrie swallowed hard to keep from gagging at the thought.

"But that's not all," Nate added.

"There's more than that?" Vi asked.

"I have to paint the words DEATH TO ALL JEWS on their door with black paint."

"You can't do that," Vi said. "That's not the Levinskys' garage. It belongs to Jonathan Carruthers, and he's our neighbor."

"That's what I said to Sonny. He just said they should have known better than to hire a Jew in the first place." Nate heaved a sigh, and his shoulders sagged. "Anyway, if I don't do it, they say they'll beat me up. And if I don't do it, someone else will. Someone who's not afraid to do it."

Garvey stepped closer to his friend. "We need to tell someone, Nate," he said. "We need help in this."

"No one can help me. I'm in too deep." In his frustration, Nate reached out and gave Garvey a hard shove. As he did, they both got off balance and tumbled down. Nate fell hard against the flat-topped trunk.

"Clumsy oaf," he said as he pulled himself up. Then he stopped cold. "Oh my. Look here."

They looked at the old trunk. The stubborn, rusty lock had fallen to the floor.

CHAPTER 17

Foiled Plan

Nate reached down to lift the trunk lid, which was finally free. Looking at Carrie, he said, "Here you go, Carrie. You always wondered what was in this thing."

He gently lifted out three silk dresses in bright blues and greens. "Just more clothes," he said in a disappointed tone.

Vi peered over his shoulder. "No, look. There's more. I see a candlestick." She knelt beside him and lifted up the tarnished silver candlestick to show the others.

"Why, that's a menorah," Carrie told them.

"A what?" Nate asked.

"I remember," Vi said. "Dvora told about it when she gave her talk. . . ." Then she stopped and looked at Carrie.

Carrie came to the trunk and looked inside, as well. "There's a dreidel," she said. "The top that Jewish children play with during Hanukkah. And here's a leather phylactery, which they call a *tefillin*. It contains verses from scripture, and the men wear it when they pray."

Nate's eyes were wide. "You mean this is a Jew's stuff? What would a Jew's stuff be doing in Aunt Oriel's attic?"

"I have no idea," Carrie said. She reached down and took out a small book. "This is the *Haggadah*, the book for the home Passover service. Dvora has one like this."

She opened the cover and saw the inscription written in old-fashioned, flowing penmanship. She read it out loud: *"To my little jewel, my delight, my little lioness of Yahweh, my Ariel. Love from Papa Yusef."*

"Papa Yusef?" Nate was shaking his head. "What is all this?"

"Look," said Vi. "Something fell out of the book." From the floor beside Carrie's feet, she picked up an old photograph. It was an unmistakable photo of a very young—and very lovely—Oriel Simmons.

Vi drew in a deep breath. "Why, this is Aunt Oriel. And look how beautiful she was." Turning it over, she said, "Aunt Oriel's real name is Ariel, and she's Jewish!"

"Then that means. . . ," Garvey said.

"That Sonny is Jewish, as well," Nate finished for him.

"Why didn't she ever tell anyone?" Vi asked.

"It's getting late," Carrie said, grabbing the Haggadah and the photo. "Come on." She headed for the stairway.

"Where are we going?" Nate demanded.

"To talk to your Aunt Oriel!"

"What if she doesn't want to talk to us?" Vi said as the four of them tramped down the narrow stairs.

"We're not asking," Carrie said. "There's not enough time to ask."

They made a stop in the kitchen to grab Opal, then hurried down the hallway to the east wing and knocked on the drawing-room door.

"What's this all about?" Opal asked.

"You'll see soon," Nate said.

When they heard Mrs. Simmons's answer to the knock, Nate pushed open the sliding mahogany doors. Opal stayed by the door-way as the four friends walked over to where the older woman was sitting in a rocking chair by the window.

Carrie had no idea how Mrs. Simmons would react to their discovery, but to her surprise, the woman seemed greatly relieved. Her slender hands relaxed into the lap of her black dress.

"Well, well, at long last," she said. "After all these years of waiting and hiding. After all these years of shame and regret, it's finally out."

"You mean you really, truly are a Jewish lady?" Nate said with a note of wonderment in his voice.

"Yes, Nathaniel, I most certainly am. Years ago, when I met your uncle James Simmons back East, even though he was a Gentile, I fell in love with him. Back in those days, there were prejudices against Jews." Then she added sadly, "There have always been prejudices against the Jews."

She gazed out the window as though to collect her thoughts. "When I married a Gentile, my family acted as though I no longer existed. James asked me to come to Minneapolis with him and not tell anyone of my heritage."

She cradled the Haggadah and the photo lovingly in her hands. "I even changed my name from Ariel, which is Hebrew for *lioness of God.*

"Every Sabbath and every Holy Day," she continued sadly, "I had to deny myself and my heritage. Although I loved James very much and I loved my children very much, I felt as though I were only half a person."

She paused, so Nate explained to her how the lock had been accidentally knocked off the trunk.

"No, Nathaniel," his aunt said. "It was no accident. The Lord used this so I could at last be honest about my past."

Carrie realized it was getting darker outside. Nate had said if he didn't do the awful deed to the Levinskys, someone else would. Carrie could barely imagine what kind of shock a bloody chicken on the doorstep would be to poor Dvora.

"Mrs. Simmons," Carrie said, "your Jewish neighbors who live next door in the garage apartment are in a great deal of danger tonight."

Mrs. Simmons immediately straightened. "The Levinskys? What kind of danger?"

They left it to Nate to explain the whole mess to his aunt. When he was finished, she gave him a long, hard look. "You are mixed up in all this Klan business?"

Nate nodded. "I'm so sorry now. I wish I'd never gone to even one meeting with Sonny."

His aunt put her hand gently on his shoulder. "My child, you have been so neglected, and it's all my fault. But things are going to be different now."

Looking at Carrie, she said, "Your father is with the newspaper, is he not?"

Carrie nodded. "Yes, ma'am, he is."

"Telephone him immediately and get him over here with a team of reporters."

"Right away." As Carrie ran out the door of the drawing room, she noticed Opal standing there with her eyes wide and her mouth gaping open.

"Well, I never in all my born days. . . ," Opal said.

Just after midnight, a handful of Klan members came to the Levinskys'. They were halfway up the stairs of the apartment, when suddenly a searchlight flooded the place and flashbulbs went off like giant lightning bugs.

Carrie's father had rigged up a radio set that amplified his voice. Over the microphone, his voice boomed out: "Klansmen, this is your only warning. Leave these premises now and never set foot on this property ever again, or you will face immediate arrest."

At that same moment, Mr. Carruthers stepped out from behind his garage. Beside him stood Dr. Kenneth Constable and Hans Maurer. A dead chicken and a bucket of paint went flying as the startled would-be raiders turned and fled.

The children had a ringside seat in the turret, where they watched every detail. And Dvora was right with them! They laughed as they saw the white-robed Klansmen running away like frightened white rabbits.

After things had calmed down some, Dvora said, "I am not surprised by the cruelty of men. I have seen much of that in my life. But never have I seen people come to my aid to stop the cruelty." Her eyes were filled with tears. "It is too amazing for words."

Carrie put her arm about her friend. "It's all right to cry," Carrie told her. "We're all your friends here."

Nate couldn't stop looking at the scene below them. "They're not so tough, are they?" he said.

"Not at all," Garvey said. "But," he added, "I'm still glad I was up here and not down there."

"Me, too," Nate agreed. "Me, too."

CHAPTER 18

A Time to Part

"What did Sonny say when he learned he was Jewish?" Father asked Carrie at the breakfast table a couple days later.

"Vi said he was pretty shocked at first."

"I would think so," Mother put in. "Especially after he'd been taught by the Klan to hate them so."

"He and his grandmother have been spending long hours together talking in her drawing room," Carrie told them. She recalled the glow in Violet's eyes as her friend talked about it. Mrs. Simmons told the children that she would hide no longer—that they would all become a loving family. Violet and Nate were overjoyed.

"Did the housekeeper know that Mrs. Simmons was Jewish?" Father asked.

Carrie shook her head. "She didn't. She was just as surprised as the rest of us."

"Well," Mother said as she put slices of bread in the electric toaster, "I'm certainly glad you knew what those items were when the trunk was opened."

"And it was all because of Dvora that I did know," Carrie said.

"Didn't you tell me the grandson—what's his name? Sonny?— is interested in radios?" Father asked.

Carrie nodded. "In his basement shop, he has a radio set and dozens of books about radios. Recently he started working at a radio shop downtown."

"I wonder if he'd be interested in a job at a real radio station."

"Father, do you mean it?" Carrie said. "You'd hire Sonny to work at the radio station? Even after what he's done with the Klan and all?"

"From what I've seen, I don't believe he was ever a full-fledged follower. Besides, everything is changed in his life now."

"That's true," Carrie said.

"We'll be needing young men who have a talent for that sort of thing. Obviously, Sonny has the talent. Will you be going over there today?"

"Yes, sir."

"You can tell Sonny that if he's interested, he should come see me at my office at the *Tribune*."

Carrie jumped up from the table. "I sure will."

"Just a minute, young lady," Mother said. "You need to finish your breakfast."

"But I'm too excited," Carrie protested.

As she grabbed her coat and hat and books, she heard Father say, "Oh, let her go, Ida. She has every right to be excited!"

"Do you have everything?" Carrie asked Dvora. They looked around the small apartment. As usual, it was so clean you could eat off the floor.

"I think so." Dvora's small bag sat by the door. "After all, I certainly didn't have much when I arrived."

"But you have acquired a few things since then."

Dvora smiled. "I sure have." She walked over to the corner and picked up Vanya. "More than you will ever know."

It was the last of February, and Dvora was leaving to go live with a Jewish family. Uncle Yerik felt that would be best for her.

"There will be many other Jewish families in the area," Dvora explained. "And Jewish children at my school. In this new neighborhood, I will attend Synagogue every Sabbath."

"I'm so happy for you," Carrie said. "And your new family wants you to bring Vanya along?"

Dvora nodded. "Yes. The cat, they said, is most welcome."

Dvora's babushka was packed away in her travel bag. She no longer wore it every day. She had told Carrie that one day when she was betrothed, she would wear it once again. But not now.

"Mrs. Simmons has been over to see me several times since the night of the Klan raid. She is such a fine lady."

"Dvora, did you know all along that Mrs. Simmons was Jewish?"

Dvora nodded. "Certainly."

"How did you know?"

"She came to me one day when I was at the garden gate playing with Vanya. She touched me and said, 'Doosh-sheesh-ka.' "

"She said it to you on the way to the vet's, as well, didn't she?"

"Yes, she did."

"What does it mean?"

"A Yiddish term. A loving, endearing term. Something my own mama might have said to me. It means *my little soul*."

Carrie remembered the day when she saw Mrs. Simmons go out of the house to visit with her little Jewish neighbor. How that must have made the lady long to acknowledge her heritage.

"I will miss you, Dvora," Carrie said, swallowing over a growing lump in her throat.

"And I will miss you, too, my friend. Tell Mrs. Harwell good-bye for me, and please take good care of the special bird feeder."

"Will I see you again, Dvora?"

"Uncle Yerik tells me that I am such a good housekeeper, he may want me to return once a week to clean house for him."

"I will see you again then," Carrie said.

"I am sure of it."

Carrie heard a car drive up. "That must be your ride. I'll help with your bag, and you carry Vanya."

Carrie opened the door and allowed Dvora to go first. There, at the bottom of the stairs, stood Violet, Nate, Sonny, Garvey, and Mrs. Simmons. Behind them stood Opal, dimples showing in her round face. When Dvora appeared, they all gave a rousing cheer. Vi and Nate held a big sign that said, "WE LOVE YOU, DVORA. WE'LL MISS YOU."

Dvora stopped and stared. She looked back up at Carrie standing behind her. Tears shone in her eyes. "This is too much for me, Carrie. My heart cannot hold all this love."

On down she went, clutching her cat and hugging each person in turn, even Garvey and Nate and Sonny. She walked to the car and crawled inside. Carrie put the bag in with her.

As the car drove away, they all waved and cheered until it vanished from their sight.

CHAPTER 19

Tune In Again Tomorrow

"Be quiet, everyone," Garvey ordered. "If you keep talking, we're going to miss it."

Vi and Nate were with Garvey and Carrie at Garvey's house. They were gathered on the floor in front of the radio console.

Carrie's heart was pounding like a bass drum. She could hardly breathe. A children's program was just over, and now it was time for the commercial.

The check from the purchase of her jingle had arrived a week ago, and Father agreed that she could split it with Garvey and give some to Dvora, as well.

"Shh, shh," Vi said, even though no one was talking.

Lively bouncy music sounded over the speaker. Then high female voices chimed in at just the right moment:

Popsicles, Popsicles—my best pick,
Flavored ice stuck on a stick.
It cools me off in the summer heat;
The yummy flavor is nice and sweet.
Oh, the joy of a Popsicle's hard to beat.

Suddenly Carrie began to laugh. She could hardly believe it was her words they were singing. She was rolling on the floor in a fit of giggles. Vi caught the giggles, and she began to laugh along with Carrie.

Garvey jumped up and began to dance a jig, singing, "Popsicles, Popsicles—my best pick, flavored ice stuck on a stick."

Now Nate was giggling, too. He and Garvey danced wildly about the room singing, "It cools me off in the summer heat; the yummy flavor is nice and sweet."

Carrie and Vi, in the midst of their giggles, chimed in on the last line, "Oh, the joy of a Popsicle's hard to beat."

Now the four of them were laughing so hard they could barely get the words out.

Aunt Frances came to the door and watched them for a minute. She shook her head and muttered, "Is this what radio's doing to this younger generation?"

"Tune in tomorrow: same time, same station," Carrie said.

Garvey answered, "Righto, Jake!"

Aunt Frances went back down the hall, leaving a chorus of giggles behind her.